FINDING MARIAN

ALSO BY NANCY PATTERSON

The Carving Place

The Bargain, Paulette's Story

(Author's Note: It is recommended that the books in this series be read in the order listed above. Books can be read as a stand-alone work, but will contain spoilers.)

DEDICATION

There are numerous searches that play out in this book. Whether our characters are resolving their relationship, solving a decades-old cold case, or learning more about local lore and history, the search process is an adventure.

I dedicate this third book to all the experts in West Virginia who gave me the inside story of some of West Virgina's more famous monsters and aliens.

See more about these new friends from a far in the Credits section.

FINDING MARIAN

*A Novel
Book 3,
The Carving Place Series*

Nancy D. Patterson

LAUREL ROSE PUBLISHING
Senatobia, MS

FINDING MARIAN

This story is a work of fiction. All characters and events are products of the author's imagination. Any resemblance to any person, living or dead, is coincidental unless otherwise noted.

Documentation on the legends and myths of West Virginia can be found in the Acknowledgements section at the back of the book.

Native West Virginia artist Patty Hendricks Wolford generously gave me permission to use her abstract Mothman drawing on the cover of the book.

FINDING MARIAN

FOREWARD
January 1998
Lora Sinclair

I'm sitting in the window seat of the plane, leaving my home in Mississippi and heading back to West Virginia. I reach for Sam's hand. He gives me a wink and squeezes back. He must know the turmoil that is going on in my head.

When I left West Virginia, I thought I was going to my family homeplace to attend the wedding of my dear family friend Buck Toliver. I also wanted Sam to see where I come from—not just the land itself, but the people, the culture, the landscape, and the feel of the hill country of Mississippi.

I'm returning with the knowledge that I have a brother that I have loved my whole life as a friend. When Buck's mother, Paulette Toliver Greer told me her story, I found a new perspective on my father and our family. In many ways it made me love him more.

Watching the earth from this vantage point, all my worries seem to diminish. The patchwork of green and brown squares of crop land, roads and pastures, are hidden in the January snow.

The grant to compare cultural similarities between Appalachia and the South played out before I'd completed my research. So, what do I do now? Hopefully, something will come along. I still help Buck manage Sinclair Farm in Mississippi. Sometimes it's not easy doing that long distance from West Virginia.

So, I'm returning to this land of blue mist over the mountains, and lush green woodlands dripping with dew and rain where I found Sam Wood, a gentle man who wins my heart over and over again. When he came striding into the old store to pick me up the day I arrived in West Virginia, I was immediately at ease.

Over time and many meals, late-night talks, and acts of comfort when I needed it, I learned of his truly sweet nature. He teaches history at the local high school, and in his spare time, he carves. This man promotes the arts in West Virginia every chance he gets.

My landlady Helen has turned into a genuine friend. She's a resource for subjects that interest me, she shares her home with me, and she is a great listener. Helen lost her husband Steve recently, and she left their beautiful retreat in the mountains to return to a family home in town. Too many memories haunted her in the cabin.

Sounds like I'm talking myself into moving back into my upstairs room at Helen's house until I can sort all this out. Right now, I feel like I could sleep about a week.

Sam nudges me and kisses my cheek. "We are almost ready to land," he says. I gather my things and wait for the plane to drop its wheels and come to a stop in West Virginia.

CHAPTER 1
January 1998
Lora Sinclair

Before I can get to the front door, Helen meets me on the sidewalk and takes one of my bags. "Oh, come in and tell me all about the wedding," she says. Something in my face made her stop mid-sentence.

"Did it not go well?"

"It was beautiful—light dusting of snow, candles in the window, bride and groom beautiful and happy."

"Then what is the matter?"

"Let me get my things put upstairs, that is, if I'm welcome to move back in for a while. Then we will sit and talk."

"Of course, you can move back in. I missed you more than I ever meant to," she says, smiling.

I go upstairs where I rent a small bedroom and have access to the bathroom. Unpacking my clothes, I notice the Atlas on my desk. That's where I first saw the initial "V" scrawled on the title page. Buck and I have come full circle since I first saw that mark. I never would have imagined its true meaning.

After I put away my things and run a brush through my hair, I go downstairs where I find Helen sitting in the living room with her feet tucked underneath her while she sipps coffee from her mother's favorite china cup.

"Are you ready for the story?" I ask, with a twinkle in my eye.

"Sure am." She pats the couch next to her and hands me a steaming cup of coffee.

And so I begin my story.

We were still sitting there when her mantle clock chimed 11 p.m. I told her everything, from how Sam and I carved on my tree, to the fun I had helping Simsie and Buck decorate the old church, to meeting Buck's mother Paulette, and learning what all those carved "V's" that I found at home really meant.

Helen let me talk until I ran out of breath and story.

"How do you feel about all that?" she asked. "I mean about Buck."

"It makes me love him more," I told her. "He's always been like a brother. I just don't understand why no one ever told me. Did Asa think I couldn't handle all that information?"

She smiles. I felt calmer just telling someone about this twist in my life.

"The way I see it, you have a brother and a helper at the farm—someone who loves it as much as you do," she said.

"I guess you're right. It was just a shock. I'm glad to be back here. I'll just try to calm down and see what life brings. I was really glad Sam went with me."

"Me too," she said smiling. We drank our coffee and enjoyed each other's company without too much chatter. That comfortable silence is a sign of true friendship.

CHAPTER 2
Sam

To tell you the truth, I was a little disappointed that Lora wanted to go back to Mrs. Wilmer's house. I really expected her to settle in here with me. I know she cares deeply for me. Maybe I need to tell her just how much I do love her.

When she is here with me, dancing around the kitchen, sitting on the deck with Goose the lab, rocking in the big wooden chair in the kitchen with her feet by the stove while she reads —it just feels so right. She leaves a big hole when she's not here.

But speaking of Goose, he was so glad to see me he almost knocked me down with joy when he bounded out of my friend Rex's truck. He whimpered and barked and licked.

I finally got him to settle down. When he realized I was home he plopped down in front of the stove while Rex and I talked in the kitchen. My friend has fought some serious depression and substance abuse issues this past year. That's not uncommon in these parts.

I find it hard to be depressed when I'm surrounded by nature, the lake out back, and the magnificence of the mountains in the distance. But to some, I guess the isolation of being here in the mountains can be lonely. Anyway, Rex got help and is doing better. He helps his mother, Mrs. Josie, run the main general store in town. It was good for him to have the company of Goose while I was away. Maybe I should talk to him about getting a dog of his own, like the chocolate lab he once had.

After taking off a few days from teaching, I'm sure I have stacks of paperwork to catch up on. It's never easy as a school teacher to return after an absence. I'm not sure what my substitute teacher had those kids doing.

I've had a hard time keeping the attention of some of my seventh graders lately. That's a hard age. The guys want to be tough, but their voices are going up and down, and most of the girls are taller than they are. In class, they are bored.

I have an idea of something that might pique their interest and be fun for Lora and me too. West Virginia is supposed to be one of the most haunted states in the country. Maybe I could include a ghost story or two in my lecture.

It might be best to give Lora a few days to rest and recover before I pick up where we left off. She has decisions to make—about whether to stay here or go home. If she goes back to Mississippi, I might have decisions to make.

CHAPTER 3
Tony and Al

Al and I drive slowly up the mountainous Curly Willow Road. After all these years, the county decided it was time for central heat and air in the old church up here. Since the church is on some kind of historical register, the county took over management from the last group that was there on a full-time basis. The congregation, I hear, has dwindled. Some of them are in their 60s, but most are older. No telling what we will have to dig through to install duct work.

We pull up in front of the Curly Willow Creek Church. It sits at the end of this winding road. Built in 1880, the old building is now home to a small Methodist congregation with a visiting preacher who holds services there on Sundays. There is no full-time staff in place there. I understand that the church is used for weddings and funerals, and for other events. It has been home to several denominations over the years.

The nearby creek and the community bear the name Curly Willow for the beautiful and contorted branches of a species of Willow trees that grow near the creek. That particular tree isn't too hardy. Ladies from the congregation have kept the stand of trees by the creek replanted and cared for.

Local artisans used the branches in floral arrangements, in furniture making, and other types of primitive art.

I turn off the truck and we just sit and take in the scene—red brick, two story building, with a tower and some influence of gothic architecture in the shapes of the leaded glass windows. Nothing too fancy, but beautiful. A small cemetery surrounded by a low iron fence, sits to the side of the church. The ground is rough around the church yard with outcroppings of stone scattered here and there.

"Hey Al, didn't your granddaddy go to this church years ago?" I ask as we start gathering our supplies out of the back of my old Chevy truck. The road up here was just wide enough for one vehicle. I didn't know what we would have done if we had met another car or truck in some of the narrow places.

"Yep, sure did," says Al. "He and my grandma went here. After she died, he just quit coming. He went every now and then to a church in town. It was just easier."

"It looks like the grass has been mowed. There is probably a group of men from the church that volunteer to help with the upkeep," I tell Al who is rustling around in his lunch sack for a snack. "Man, we just got here. It's going to be a long day if you start eating your lunch now."

He grins and digs out a cupcake.

"Let's see what we have to do." We head up the walkway to the church.

I turn the key in the heavy lock of the big, wooden door. The electricity is on, so we flip the switches, and the lights flicker and then come on. They look like old gas fixtures that were converted to electricity. The floor is made of wide-plank pine that squeaks in several places as we walk toward the alter.

There are two small rooms on one side of the sanctuary. I suppose those are for Sunday School or meetings. At the back is a small room that serves as a library and office. A small hall behind the office, we discover, leads to a staircase that goes to the tower.

Besides a basement that hasn't been used for anything for years, there's not much else to see.

"We can run the duct work in the main part of the church through the basement and put the vents in the floor," says Al.

"Let's see if we can use the room in the tower to get air to the small balcony area below," I say as we head back to the closet and the staircase. The stairs make about three turns to get you to the room above. When you stand in the middle of the small space, you can see the countryside for miles.

Beneath the tall windows are window seats with hinged tops for storage. I am busy looking at the scenery below when I hear papers shuffling. Al is sitting cross-legged on the floor pulling out boxes of papers and other assorted, old documents.

"What in the world are you doing, Al?" I say, bending over to see what he's gotten into.

"There are a bunch of boxes in the window seats all along that East wall," says Al. "We will have to move all this stuff before we can start measuring to see if the ductwork will fit."

"Ok. Let's see if we can move it downstairs while we are working up here."

Al and I started moving the boxes in the

window seats. Most were in heavy cardboard boxes containing old church bulletins and other church-related documents. We were careful to stack them in order when we moved them to a downstairs closet. The last box was a heavier cardboard box that held files, folders, and a thin, white, cardboard shirt box tied with string.

Al picked it up and it literally fell apart. Tumbling out of the box was a large scrap of material, possibly part of a child's dress. The six-inch scrap looked like it was torn from a garment. It was mainly light brown with yellow and green flowers on it. Maybe it came from the hem of the dress since it was edged in lace, once white, now discolored. Most of the scrap was stained dark brownish red. It looked like blood.

"Don't touch it, Al. We need to put that stuff back where it was and call the sheriff and let him decide what to do with it. This is county property, after all."

Tony carefully files the contents back in the box. "Hey most everything I've seen is about a missing little girl back in 1959—Marian Atchley. Ever heard anything about that?'

"Yeah, I have. It's kind of local lore around here. What did you read?"

"The boxes are full of newspaper clippings

about it. I didn't read all of them, just looked at the headlines. Looks like some bigger papers in the state picked up the story, too."

After shutting the box that held the scrap and straightening the mounds of papers and newspapers, we put all the boxes and the shirt box back in the window seat. There was a phone in the church office. We headed down the narrow stairs to make the call.

"Sheriff Jackson, please," I said into the receiver.

"One moment," said the dispatcher.

I held my hand over the mouthpiece of the phone. "Al, I've known Will Jackson and his family all my life. I believe he is a good man and will do some investigating of all that stuff up there…"

"Jackson here."

"Hey there Will. This is Tony. Al and I are out here at the church at Curly Willow Creek to see about installing air conditioning as the county requested."

"Yeah," said the sheriff. "You got a problem?"

"We were in the tower to look at spaces that might work for installing duct work. Opened one of those window seats and came across some things you might be interested in."

"Oh, yeah? Like what?"

"Old documents, photographs from the 1950s and a piece of what could be from a little girl's dress. And it is covered in blood."

Jackson had been clicking his ink pen in frustration, waiting for me to quit bothering him. When I mentioned the dress, the clicking stopped. There was silence.

"What did you do with that stuff, Tony?"

"Oh, we put it back just like we found it, in the window seat. Do you...."

Jackson interrupted. "Just leave it there. I'll check it out next time I'm up there. Why don't y'all just close up the church and knock off for the day?"

"Sure thing." I heard the connection break.

"That was kinda strange," I told Al, who had been listening to my side of the conversation. "Guess we have the day off. I'll call the county office and tell them what's going on."

We locked up and got in our work truck for the drive down the mountain, back to town. "Al, I guess you can go ahead and eat the rest of your lunch."

Neither of us had much to say as we rode with the windows down letting the mountain air rush in.

CHAPTER 4
Lora

I don't know why I can't commit wholeheartedly to Sam. He's all I ever dreamed of. I guess growing up like I did, with a blended family and no mother, I learned to set limits for myself. If I rode my tricycle on a sidewalk, there was one particular block in the walk that I couldn't or wouldn't go past. I had to go to town to the library parking lot to ride my tricycle because there wasn't any concrete at the farm.

My Aunt Shelly took me about once a week after she picked me up from school. Shelly was a big part of my life. After my mother died when I was three, Shelly came to live with us and help out with me. As my mother's younger sister, she was about 18 when she came to the farm. She had just finished high school and put off college until I was 10 and could pretty much fend for myself.

Even in my partying days during and after college, I set limits. While the other girls were getting plastered at parties, I knew where the stopping point for me was. It was just when I felt my self-control beginning to slip.

I couldn't get too close to any of my friends. I was afraid they would leave or betray me. So, I limited myself to casual friendships—just before I was on the brink of being hurt if they moved away or decided to run with another crowd.

I suppose that's what I'm doing with Sam, and it's not fair to him.

Tomorrow I'm going to investigate some job possibilities. I think I need to stay up here until I'm surer about what I want and how I feel.

The second day after I came back, I started unpacking and putting things back where they had been before I left for Mississippi—jeans and shirts in the wardrobe, books on the small antique desk. Without saying it outload, I must feel like I'll be here for a while. It is a week until spring break, and Sam will be out of school. Maybe he can help me come up with some ideas for a job. Maybe he can show me parts of West Virginia that I still haven't seen.

It's almost dark and I find myself sitting on

Sam's back deck staring at a candle he has placed in the center of a small wrought iron table. When I look up, the sky has darkened more that I'd realized. He is busy in the kitchen. I stare at the candle and the silvery moths that hover in the light.

"What 'cha doing?" Sam says as he rubs my shoulders.

"Oh, just watching candle flippers. That's what my daddy called the moths."

'Speaking of moths, have you ever heard about our legend of the Mothman?" He has a mischievous look in his eyes.

"What?" I said, laughing while he pretended to be serious.

"No, really. In 1966 and 1967, there were reports of a man-size being with a huge wing spread and glowing red eyes, hovering in the sky near Point Pleasant. Some believe it appears as an omen right before a disaster."

"Are you serious?" I asked beginning to wonder what in the world Sam was talking about.

"Yeah, kids said they saw the creature. The news media picked up the story and it's been legend in these parts since then.

"A professor at the local university theorized that what had been seen was actually a sandhill crane.

It was a huge gray bird with red feathering around its eyes. Another law enforcement theory was that it was a kind of heron.

"West Virginia is known as the most haunted state. Hey, I have an idea. When I'm off for spring break, why don't I take you to some of the places where these ghost/monster stories originated?"

"You sound like you've been lecturing on this in class. Have you?" I asked, noting his enthusiasm on the subject.

I could tell Sam was excited about this subject. "Well, not yet, but I've been making some notes. I might be able to work it into the West Virginia history class.

"There is a woman at the university who I've been wanting to talk to. She is somewhat of an expert on local myths, legends, and lore. Maybe if we are in that area, I could see her. Then again, she might not want to interrupt her spring break to talk to me. I'll write to her this week to see if she can work me into her schedule."

I have to admit, that sounds fun and interesting. I will do a little research, myself, and see if it's worth investigating. It might turn into a three- or four-part story. Maybe I could sell the idea to the newspaper or a West Virginia tourism publication.

I couldn't help myself. The wheels in my head were turning fast, and the idea of spending a few days on the road with Sam was pretty exciting, too.

CHAPTER 5
Claudia Watson

I'm the dispatcher for the county Sheriff's Office. I've been working here close to 40 years—first for Frank Jackson, who was the sheriff in the 1950s and early '60s. Now I work for his son Will.

The sheriff is at his desk after talking with Tony Bramlett. He is staring at the window in his office, but I bet he's not seeing a thing.

Will had told me that he remembered his mother talking about a case in 1959. She said it had unnerved Frank so much that he did not run for reelection when his term was up. The case involved the abrupt disappearance of a five-year-old girl, Marian Atchley. Her family lived near the Curly Willow Creek community.

Reports said that Marian was playing outside

the family's modest home. She had a new puppy and was last seen making a leash out of braided hay strings for the dog—a mixed breed that looked like it may have been a shepherd-mutt cross.

Marian's dad was working in the mines. Her mother was in the house doing routine household chores. When she opened the door to call Marian for lunch, she was nowhere to be seen. The pup was sitting near the old cedar in the front yard wearing his new partially-braided leash.

The older Sheriff Jackson had organized a search party. They spent two weeks combing the mountain area of Curly Willow Creek. Men on horses and search and rescue dogs covered the nearby woods. Women at the church made hand-lettered flyers that were posted in town and nearby communities.

Nothing. No sign of a struggle in the yard, no footprints, no scratches or marks on the puppy. Marian's mother was interviewed over and over. No enemies, no strangers in the area, nothing heard outside. Marian was five-years-old, had long brown hair pulled back with a green ribbon, light blue eyes. She was wearing worn brown shoes and a brown dress with little yellow and white flowers on it. Her mother had sewn it by hand using material from an old dress of her own. Her case was never solved and remained open.

Sheriff Frank Jackson never quit thinking about possibilities, never quit hoping for clues, never let a day go by that it didn't come to the surface of his thoughts. Two years after he retired as sheriff, he died of pneumonia leaving a wife and a young son, Will.

There have been other men to hold the office between Frank's departure and Will's being sworn in after the recent election. Of the two Jackson men, Will is my favorite. He's not your typical county sheriff. He is a big man with the looks of an athlete. At 6'2", Will has almost black hair, which is combed back and a neatly trimmed beard. When he turns to face you with his startling blue eyes, he commands attention.

At 38, he is probably the one of the youngest law enforcement officers in this part of West Virginia. I've seen him struggle with taking charge of deputies 10 years or more older than he is. They soon learned that he means business but is generally easy-going and smart.

Will is not the only one who has faced struggles. When Sheriff Frank Jackson hired me right after two years of college, it was 1959—the year the girl disappeared. I was barely 21. In that day it was unheard of for a young black woman to be hired in law enforcement. It was my job to be the dispatcher and occasionally ride with our only full-time deputy.

When Frank Jackson left the Sheriff's Office in 1962, he left his son with tales of his law enforcement victories. According to Will's mother, his father suffered with the unsolved case. It weighed heavily on his heart.

With Will's family background, he knows more about this county than a newcomer would. By listening to his conversation with Tony, I knew he would be going up that mountain real soon to check out that report.

CHAPTER 6
Sam Wood – Early March 1998

Lora sits cross legged in the big, wooden rocking chair next to my kitchen fireplace. Sticking out from the legs of her jeans, I see a pair of my gray, wool socks.

"I see that someone has invaded my sock drawer again." I say playfully as I pinch her sock-enclosed toe. The socks are too big, so when I try to pinch, I only get sock. "You look like an elf in those big socks."

We have a comfortable banter of conversation.

"Hey, Sam," she says, still staring into the fire. "Are you really going to take me on the ghost tour Spring Break? You know that's only a few days away."

"As a matter of fact, I am, my darling," I say in my best affected British accent. "Come see what I have over here on the table." She shuffles over to my primitive farm kitchen table which is covered with documents and maps.

"We will start in Morgantown, home of West Virginia University where I'll try to arrange a meeting with our expert on ghosts and monsters in West Virginia." I wiggle my eyebrows and twirl the ends of my imaginary handlebar mustache, making her laugh.

"But before we leave here we have to go to the courthouse," I said, continuing my travel itinerary.

"What's at our courthouse?"

"That's where you apply for a marriage license," I said, never looking her in the eye.

"Did you know that you can apply for a marriage license, wait for it to be processed, and BAM, you can get married the same day. No waiting period, no blood test."

I finally got the nerve to look up at her as she stood at my shoulder. There was definitely a look of complete shock on her face.

I dropped to my knees in front of her. "Lora Sinclair, I have never met anyone like you. I have carved my initials on your name tree in Mississippi, I have loved you since I picked you up at the old store the day you came to West Virginia, and I want you to marry me. We will have a glorious life, here or Mississippi or where ever the wind takes us."

She smiles and sank to her knees too. "Sam, I know I have held back some in our relationship. I guess I couldn't believe someone like you really existed." She kissed me sweetly. "After we get married can we go on our monster tour and return in time to get you back to school?

"You bet, baby. I can't believe you said yes!"

Still reeling from shock and happiness, we spread out all the maps and documents on the table.

"We can start in Morgantown and try to see the expert lady, and maybe she will tell us about the ghosts and monsters of West Virginia. I've even heard that some spirits live at the University. Then we will head to Flatwoods near Sutton to check out he Flatwoods Monster, also known as Braxie and the

Green Monster. He is supposed to look like an alien and has a body type that doesn't resemble a human form.

She looks at me with squinting eyes and a slight smile on her face.

"Then to Point Pleasant to see the top West Virginia monster, The Mothman. He is really cool."

I tackled her to the wide pine planks of the cabin floor.

"And we will honeymoon all the way across the state." She giggled, sweetly.

"Where will we live, what will we do for money…" she said dramatically with the back of her hand pressed to her forehead. I covered her mouth with my hand.

"We have time to work all that out later."

"Tell me more ghost stories."

CHAPTER 7
Lora Sinclair

I'm driving back to my place at Helen's, down the mountain. I can't wait to tell her my news. There is a certain inner peace settling inside me. Seeing Sam so happy made me happy.

I guess that means that we will go to the courthouse in a day or two and then take off on our monster tour.

Helen is in the kitchen when I come in, letting the screen door slam behind me. She knows just by looking at my face that I'm bubbling with news.

We pull up chairs to the kitchen and I share my news.

"I'm so happy for you, Lora," she says. "But I'm sad for me. I hate to lose a good renter."

"Oh, you won't lose me. We don't know where we can live. Sam's cabin is great, but it's a little small for both of us and Goose. I do think we will stay here in West Virginia for the time being. I'll still have to make trips to Mississippi to check on Buck and Simsie and the farm."

Buck and his new bride Simsie, are living in our family's old farmhouse at Sinclair Farm, back at the small community, known as Crossroads.

Helen bit her lower lip and looked a little distracted.

"What's wrong, Helen?"

"Oh, nothing. I've had this idea for some time, but I didn't want to mention it to you until you and Sam were married. I saw it coming all along."

"What?"

"Why don't you and Sam move into my big cabin in the mountains? You know it is already furnished, but you could add your own touch as well. My daughter has no interest in living up here. When you move out upstairs, there will be plenty of room for her family upstairs at this house."

She paused, waiting for my reaction.

"I'm overwhelmed! Of course, I need to talk to Sam and show him the cabin. It's something I would love to consider. What about rent? Can we afford it on a teacher's salary? And I'm not even working right now."

"Lora, it will give me such peace for you and Sam to be living in the house that Steve and I built. You can enjoy the things we collected—rugs, pottery. You know that houses die when they are vacant. It will help me to have someone in it, and I know you will take care of it. Goose is over the baby lab stage of chewing, I bet he will be fine. Why don't you and Sam go look at it, and then we can talk details? By the way, I have a message for you. Sheriff Will Jackson wants you to call him." She hands me a piece of paper with his number on it.

She presses the key into my hand and gives me a nod as if to say, "It's okay. Take it."

Wow, I've had too much sprung on me at one time. I have a good, peaceful feeling about it all.

I'm at Sam's cabin when he comes home from teaching.

"Hey, are you the welcoming committee?" he says playfully, bending me backward with drama and giving me a kiss. My back makes a loud crack which breaks the romance of the moment.

"I want to take you somewhere. We've got something to think about."

We pile into his truck with Goose in the back. He is beginning to get a few gray hairs on his muzzle. I've heard that black labs go gray sooner than others. Maybe it just shows up more. He has not slowed down. If he even hears the tiny jingle of Sam's keys, he is out the door sitting by the truck, thumping his tail in the dirt and smiling.

"Where are we going?" asked Sam, with a puzzled look on his face. He looks especially good to me, typical Sam in his faded jeans, a long-sleeve shirt with the sleeves rolled up, his dark hair curling around the collar of his shirt. His stubble has almost turned into a full-fledged beard. I can't believe I get to look at his beautiful face when I wake up each morning.

I point him in the direction of Helen's cabin. I had told him about it before, but not in much detail or where is was located.

When I saw the nearly-hidden driveway, I said, "Turn here."

"Here? I don't see anything."

"You will."

We drove around a curve on what looked like a well-tended horse trail. Then the scenery broke—the mountains, the water, still a little snow tipping the evergreens. He stopped the truck outside the cabin, killed the motor, and looked at me.

"What's up?"

I showed him the key. "Helen wants us to consider living here after we are married."

He looked at me like I had sprouted a second head. "What?"

I could tell he was shutting down. He loved his little cabin, and I could understand that. "Let's just go look inside," I pleaded. "We don't have to decide right now, but I want you to see it."

Although I had been to the cabin with Helen, I tried to look at it through Sam's eyes. We opened the door and stepped inside. I watched as he took it all in. The beautiful woodwork, massive fireplace, pottery, hand-woven rugs, books, furniture, and most of all, the panoramic view looking at a breath-taking mountain scenery.

I could tell he was impressed but reserved.

"This is nothing like I expected it to be," he said with his back to me as he looked out at the magnificent view. "But all this is Helen's. It's not ours. What about our carvings, and our books and treasures?"

"Helen says we can enjoy these things or pack them up. I would hate to see Goose make an afternoon snack out of one of these rugs." As soon as

I'd said it, I knew that was a mistake.

"If Goose can't come, we can't either," he said, never turning around to look at me.

I was determined this would not be our first fight. If we both didn't want to make this move, then we would stay in his cabin.

"Sam, this is just a discussion at this point. We have so much to talk about. I'm not going to try to push you into this. I just wanted you to see the beauty out here so we could talk about the option." I sat down on the big hearth.

He finally turned and faced me. Walking over to me, I rose to meet him, and we shared a long hug.

"We will talk about all these things when we go on our monster hunt. In the meantime, we better make some plans and pack a bag," I say.

We drive back down the mountain a ways and turn in at his cabin.

"Okay, I need to go back to Helen's and start packing. When do we start this grand adventure?"

"He winks at me and leans across the truck seat for a quick kiss. How about day after tomorrow. That will give me time to pack, take Goose to Rex, get out my maps and notes and make a few phone calls. So, I was thinking, maybe we could have Rex and Helen come with us to the courthouse. What do you think?"

"What about your parents? I know you don't see them very often, but don't you think they will want to know that you're getting married?" I ask, watching his get a distant look in his eyes.

"That's one of the phone calls I need to make. I think they will be fine with not having a big deal of a wedding. I'll tell them that I'll bring you to meet them when I get out of school this summer," he says. I can tell he has given this a lot of thought.

"Okay. I have some calls to make too—to Buck and my Aunt Shelly. And for some reason, Helen says Sheriff Jackson wants me to call him. Think I'm in trouble?"

"No," he says. "Will Jackson is a good guy. Let me know what he wants after you talk to him."

I look at him and realize that I'm smiling so big it's making my cheeks hurt. "I'll see if Helen will let me in the kitchen tonight so I can make us dinner. We need to include her too."

"Alright my girl. See you soon." I hop out of the truck and get into my car to head back to start the ball rolling.

CHAPTER 8
Lora

"Sheriff's Office," says the dispatcher when I return Will Jackson's call.

"I'm Lora Sinclair. I'm returning a call from Sheriff Jackson. Is he available?"

"Sure is. One moment." She puts me on hold.

"Will Jackson," he says when he picks up the call. His voice is so deep it seems to resonate from far down in his chest.

"Yes, I'm Lora Sinclair. Helen Wilmer told me you would like to talk to me."

"Hi, Lora, thanks for calling me back. I have a case I'm working on that I need some help on. I ran into Helen the other day and she told me a little about you—your background, your museum work. I need someone that can help me to organize some material we just found that relates to an old cold case.

"Do you think you could come by this week and talk to me about the possibility of doing a little research for the department?"

I am surprised at his request. "Wow, I couldn't imagine what you might want with me. My boyfriend told me that he didn't think I was in trouble. He thinks highly of you."

"Who's your boyfriend, if you don't mind my asking?"

"Sam Wood, he teaches history at the high school…" Jackson stops me mid-sentence.

"Oh, I know Sam. Good guy. Talented too. What about day after tomorrow?"

"Oh goodness. I can't come then. In fact, Sam and I are getting married that day. It's just a simple ceremony at the courthouse. Then we are going on a little ghost hunting adventure."

Jackson laughs. His voice is deep and calm. He doesn't sound like most cops.

"Well, congratulations. Anything I can do for you, just let me know."

I think out loud. "I guess I could come tomorrow if it won't take too long."

"No, that would be great. I just need so go over

the details of the case. You'll know if it's something you would be interested in doing. What about 9 in the morning?"

"Okay with me. But, Sheriff Jackson, I don't have any law enforcement training. Why me?"

"I need a fresh set of eyes to look at this case. I have a long history with it. I also need someone with good organizational skills. If we are going to reopen the case, I need to have all the facts together in chronological order.

"I want you to compare the information we have in the records here with that in the boxes at the old church. See if there is something in one set that isn't in the other."

"Sounds interesting. Thanks for thinking of me for this job. I guess I'll see you in the morning. Oh, and please keep the wedding thing to yourself. Not many people know me here. Sam is well-known since he teaches school. I guess we are just private people. I'd appreciate it."

We ended our call. What in the world had Helen told him about me? I had to admit, I was intrigued by the little information he had given me.

CHAPTER 9
Sam

I'm packing my brown duffle with my usual attire—jeans, couple of long-sleeved shirts, notebooks, a pocket-size tape recorder for documenting my conversations with the monster experts, camera, and light jacket. Deep in the corner pocket of the bag is a blue velveteen box with a simple gold band.

This morning I called a research librarian at West Virgini University, Dr. Aleida Cutland, affectionally called "Cutty" by her colleagues and students. She has agreed to meet with us in Morgantown. I'm to call her when we get there.

My plan is for Lora and me to visit the courthouse with Helen in tow as a witness on Wednesday morning. Then we will drop off

Helen and make our way to Morgantown. I'm still surprised that Lora said "yes." I was afraid that she would need time to think about it. Her eyes said it all as soon as I asked her.

CHAPTER 10
Lora

Helen drops me off at the sheriff's office for my meeting with Will Jackson while she runs some errands. The sheriff's office is located in an old, one-story red-brick building just off Main Street.

Claudia, the dispatcher I talked to yesterday, meets me when I open the front door. She is surrounded by stacks of paperwork and radio equipment, but it is clear that she is in charge of her domain.

I introduce myself and she smiles and stands to shake my hand. The Sheriff must have heard me come in as he emerges from his small office behind Claudia's desk.

"Lora? Will Jackson," he says, extending his hand.

Jackson looks a little like I had pictured him, but I never expected those startling blue eyes. "Let's go in this little conference room," he says motioning to a room with a long wooden library table and a few metal chairs.

"I'll get right to the point. I chose you to help me based on what I learned about your museum curator experience and your reputation for research. My father struggled with the case of a missing five-year-old girl—Marian Atchley. She disappeared from her front yard at her mountain home in 1959. She was last seen playing with her new mixed-breed puppy. She was braiding a leash for him from hay strings.

"When the mother called her to come in, there was no response. The dog was sitting outside wearing his new leash. The next morning the dog was gone. My father launched a community-wide search that included men on horses, trained trackers with dogs, volunteer groups and church members from the nearby Curly Willow Creek Church where the family attended worship services.

"Nothing. Not a trace. No broken branches, no scent to follow, no sightings. There was assistance from the state and the feds. After the years went by it was just a cold case sitting in a filing cabinet.

"Until this week. I got a call from Tony Bramlett

and his partner who had been hired to install air conditioning, including duct work at the Curly Willow Creek Church. In the tower room there are window seats built in all around the small space.

"Apparently, they were considering those spaces for ductwork to the floor below. When they started moving the contents, they noticed a box, different from the others, of newspaper clippings all regarding Marian's disappearance. But most importantly, they found a smaller box that held a scrap of fabric, brown with little yellow and white flowers on it. It had stains on it that could have been blood stains. They called me."

"Why was that fabric so important?"

"It fits the description of the dress Marian was wearing when she disappeared."

Lora sat quietly taking it all in and making a few notes as he talked.

"What happened to all that stuff?"

"It is stored in an unused Sunday School room at the church. The church is small and only meets on Sunday. The heat and air work has been suspended. The group that governs activities at the church has taken any special events off the calendar. They will allow us access to go through the records."

"You want me to organize the newspaper

clippings by date?"

"Yes, that and more. As you go through them, look for any clues or details that could have been overlooked. I've sent the fabric to the state crime lab for analysis."

"You mentioned parents, are they still alive?"

"If they are, we can't locate them. We have tried. Seems they left the area not long after it was apparent that Marian was not coming home. Could be in another state, or remarried, who knows? All efforts to find them have failed."

"We will be on our little trip the rest of this week. I can get started Monday, is that alright?"

"Oh, sure. And this is a paid assignment. We don't expect you to do this work without pay."

He stood as I left the room, calling after me, "Best wishes for tomorrow."

"Thanks."

I can't wait to tell Sam about my meeting. I don't think he will have any information on this case but could have heard some town talk about it from the older folks. Tomorrow can't come soon enough.

CHAPTER 11
Lora and Sam

Our little wedding ceremony was perfect for us. We didn't need all the fuss. We went to the courthouse early Wednesday morning, got our license, and were married in the beautiful courtroom that had stood witness to hundreds of trials, many marriages, and local town meetings for over a century.

The sun came in through the 100-year-old leaded windows as we said our vows with Helen and Rex as our witnesses. Sam wore slacks and a good shirt. His beard neatly trimmed and his dark curls touching his collar.

I opted for a long gauzy skirt with an off-white peasant blouse—the same outfit I'd worn to Buck and Simsie's wedding just three months ago. The justice who married us was a kind man in his 70s with longer-than-usual white hair. He said our legal vows and then said a heart-felt prayer that made tears collect in the corner of my eyes.

And we were off, and into Sam' truck we went. Goose took up his usual residence when we are out of town with Rex. "Dogs and monsters and honeymoons don't mix," said Sam with a wink and his beautiful smile.

"I need to make a few phone calls at Helen's then I'll be ready to go," I said. Rushing to my room I reach Buck Toliver back at my homeplace at Sinclair Farm.

"Hey Buck." I am almost breathless.

"Hey there yourself, Lora. Is everything okay?"

"Well I guess so since Sam and I got married about 20 minutes ago."

"What??! I can't believe you didn't tell us."

"I'm telling you now," I say giggling. "We just decided it was time. No fuss, but I wanted you to know. Tell Simsie if I'd had a big wedding, she would have been standing right beside me."

Buck takes a big breath and lets it out.

"You aren't the only one with news. Simsie and I just found out that we are going to have a baby. How about that?"

It was my time to squeal with excitement. So many things were coming together it was making me dizzy.

"Oh, wow, that makes me an aunt. I can't wait to go shopping. Look, we will talk later. Sam is waiting for me in the truck. We are just going on a little trip for a few days. Please tell Shelly for me. Tell her not to be mad."

"How could she be? Love you Lora."

"You too Buck."

"Where now?" I asked, getting settled into my seat in the truck.

"First stop is Morgantown, a couple of hours away."

"Tell me what to expect there?"

"I'd rather you see the stately old buildings on campus first. After we meet with Dr. Cutland, there might be some tales I don't know about. For instance, there is supposed to be cat apparition in the library. I'm sure she has more.

I kick off my shoes and reach for Sam's hand. Suddenly I realize that I'm still smiling. It feels so good.

CHAPTER 12
John Tolliver (Buckshot)

We live on Sinclair Farm in Mississippi. I've been with the Sinclair family since I was 5. Mr. Asa, Lora's daddy, raised me like he was my father, and it turns out he was. I never knew it until after he died—at my wedding, in fact. It's wonderful to know you belong to a place, to a family.

When Lora moved to West Virginia, I stayed with Mr. Asa and helped with the farm. After he died, Lora asked Simsie and me to move into the house and be in charge of the daily operation of the farm.

That's a big responsibility for me. Simsie helps me when she can after work. She is a nurse, so when she gets home, she has already put in a hard day.

Lora checks behind me on the books, and we make big decisions together. I can't believe she and

Sam just up and got married without telling anyone. Well, now that I think about it, maybe I can. Lora has always been so independent. Sam is good for her. I'm glad she took that step.

My life has changed so much since I found out I was really part of this family. My mother came to the wedding, and boy did that open doors. She told Lora all about her relationship with Asa and how she left me with him because it was best for me.

Now, it's not too late to have a relationship with her—something I never had. We plan to call her soon and tell her that we are expecting a baby. Simsie wants to go to the doctor first and make sure everything is okay. I really don't know how Paulette, my mother, will take this. She was a little shy at the wedding and didn't say much.

I've gotten letters or calls from her every week since, and she has opened up. There is even a smile in her voice. I can't help hoping this is a good thing. I know I don't need to get hurt the second time around.

I guess it's time to go to work. Some spring calves are already on the ground with more to come. Sister, our border collie, goes with me every day and does her job of bunching up the herd so I can count cows. I depend on her more than I realize.

She circles the cows quiet-like and takes commands from me. I use the same ones cues that Asa taught me when I was just a kid. If she sees something new or wrong, she will drop and lay down. That's her signal for me to come check things out.

"Come on Sister. Load up." She jumps up on the truck seat beside me when I open the passenger side door. As usual, when she pants, she looks like she is smiling. I like to think she is.

CHAPTER 13
Lora and Sam

I still can't believe I'm driving down the road, listening to some song by Kris Kristofferson, and holding my bride's hand. We have about another hour before we get to Morgantown.

I have made a reservation at a historic hotel there. We can spend the night there and start our research tomorrow with Dr. Cutland.

What a place to spend your honeymoon— hunting ghosts and monsters—just right for us.

We drive into Morgantown which is one of the largest cities in the state. It was settled in late 1700s.

We drive by West Virginia University and its stately buildings. Then we find Hotel Morgan, a historic hotel that opened in 1925. We can have dinner there in its fine restaurant and begin our honeymoon. Tonight is ours. Work and touring start tomorrow.

Dr. Cutland answers her phone on the first ring.

"Dr. Cutland, this is Sam Wood. You had agreed to meet with me and my wife today. Is that still convenient?"

I can't believe that I said, "my wife." I never dreamed this would actually happen.

"Oh, yes Sam. The University is closed for the break, but I can still meet you in my office. Shall we meet outside about 10?"

"Great. I'll see you in about an hour."

CHAPTER 14
Sam and Lora

Lora and I were both excited.

I have to remind myself that I'm here to interview Dr. Cutland in order to get authentic information if I am to use this information of ghosts, monsters, and lore in my West Virginia history class. It helps that the subject has fascinated me since I was a teenager.

Lora and I drive up to our designated meeting place. Soon Dr. Cutland arrives. We make introductions and she leads us to her office, careful to unlock door and make sure they are relocked.

It always interests me how you make a mental image of someone when you talk on the phone. I expected a tall, stern woman. Instead, I found a woman, about 5 feet 2 inches tall. She is warm and friendly and loves talking about her subject matter.

"Call me Cutty. All my students do," she says smiling. When she smiles, her cheeks push her big round glasses further up her nose. Her salt and pepper hair is short and spiky.

We make ourselves comfortable in a conference room adjoining her office. The whole suite is decorated with posters of Mothman, the Green Monster, and more.

"Okay Cutty, let's start with why West Virginia is so haunted."

She takes a deep breath and settles back in a beautiful arm chair covered with worn but exotic material—gargoyles are carved into the armrests. She uses a footstool since her feet don't quite touch the floor.

I reach in my worn leather satchel and pull out a legal pad and pen and start my tape recorder after getting her permission to document our conversation.

"The obvious question is, why is West Virginia one of the most haunted places in the country?"

"There are as many reasons as tales! Settlers from Italy, China, Switzerland, who came for jobs in timber, railroads, coal, and glass brought their own folktales and legends, and many of those were retold in our local settings.

"The landscape with its mountains and hollows, is somewhat isolated. Swapping stories was a way for people from different cultures to bond, and a way to provide an evening's entertainment with little or no cost."

I glance over at Lora. She is sitting on the edge of her seat, absorbing every word.

"West Virginia has a long and rich history, and much of it involved violence, death, and mutilation. Although the poor mountain whites who drank and feuded with their neighbors are a sad and incomplete stereotype, there were many murders. The isolation along with family and regional loyalty forced the coverup of many crimes," she said, becoming more animated as she continued talking.

"Many tales were told to warn children away from danger. Parents might tell their children not to go to the river alone because a ghost might get them, hoping this would keep them from the danger of the river. Some of the waterfalls and rivers have taken many lives, and these places were sometimes considered cursed by the indigenous people. Legend has it that Chief Cornstalk cursed the area of Point Pleasant long before the Mothman sightings and accompanying disasters."

"Are there ghosts here at the university?"

"The WVU legend I have most often heard is that the painting of Elizabeth Moore moving around in E. Moore Hall."

"Who was Elizabeth Moore?" Lora asks.

"She was the principal of Woodburn Female Seminary. That was an educational academy for woman that was located in Woodburn Circle before the University was founded," says Cutty.

"She was a champion for women's rights and a mentor for her students. Many claim Moore's presence is still felt here, especially in E. Moore Hall, which bears her name.

"Some say the library is haunted by Moore's cat Sheba. She is said to guard collections in the older part of the library.

"There is also a story of Sally, who was an eight-year-old girl. She attended a party at Reynolds Hall and had a great time dancing around in her Victorian party dress. Soon after, she died during the typhoid outbreak. Facility workers report seeing a young girl in a party dress dancing around the place where she had so much fun.

"Am I going too fast for you Sam?"

I had given up on furiously taking notes and was glad I had the small recorder. I nodded to it as she talked to make sure she was aware that I was recording the conversation.

"I do need to take a break and get some water," said Cutty. She hopped down from her chair and disappeared down the hall.

"I could use something to drink, too," I said to Lora who was still posed with her chin resting on the top of her fists. She was absorbing all this like a sponge.

"Yep, me too. Let's go find some water or a drink machine and stretch our legs. Sam, I'm leaving her a note that we will be right back."

We walked down the hall, our steps echoing on the old floors. The emptiness of the building added to the creepy atmosphere we had created.

After our little break we rejoined Dr. Cutty back in the conference room.

"Would it be possible to see the portrait?" asked Lora.

"I suppose so. We will take a look. She hopped down from her chair and off we went to Elizabeth Moore Hall.

"Some say the portrait moves around, but no one admits to moving it," Cutty says as we all three stand, looking up at the elegant and aged Moore.

"Some also say her ghost is seen floating around

the swimming pool in the basement. She must be here protecting the women students."

I look down at her, into her blue eyes behind the red glasses. "Cutty, have you seen any of these things?"

"No, I haven't, but I don't make it a habit to work here at night, alone either."

"What is one of your favorite tales?"

Dr. Cutty has a twinkle in her eye when she is talking about her favorite subjects. She has settled back into her gargoyle carved chair and resumes her tales.

"I love the Greenbrier Ghost. It appears a murder victim actually provided testimony to capture her husband after he thought he had gotten away with murder. My understanding is that in an argument that started because he didn't like his dinner one evening, and wrung his wife's neck, killing her.

"He arranged what he said was her favorite scarf around her neck to hide his crime and reported her death and she was buried. Her ghost came and told her mother that her husband had killed her.

The dream repeated until the mother went to the authorities. Her body was exhumed and examined. It provided enough evidence to try and convict the husband."

"Oh, Dr. Cutty, I wish we had more time this is all so interesting," said Lora. "I suppose I need to start off this marriage being a good cook in fear of getting my neck wrung. Did Sam tell you we are on our honeymoon? We are out chasing ghosts and monsters?"

"I certainly had no idea," says Cutty, obviously delighted with the news. "I can't say I've ever had honeymoon visitors before. Let me give you another example, then you need to be on your way.

"In the next town to the South, Fairmont, there was unexplained UFO activity that contributed to the science fiction Men in Black movie that came out last year. There was an earlier book.

The theory is that these men in black suits were investigating eye witnesses of alien encounters and trying to suppress their spreading the rumors. Pop culture embraced the movie which was a big success. I even did a display case about Men in Black for the University.

"You should go. It has been delightful to meet you both. Congratulations on your recent marriage. I hope you have only fond memories of these Honeymoon days in this part of the state. You have my number. If you think of other questions, please give me a call."

With that we all left the building, and Lora and I headed for my truck. I stopped and looked back at the old buildings. They certainly look like something ghostly could reside there.

CHAPTER 15
Claudia

Will Jackson is motioning for me to come into his office. A glass window separates my space, which includes a desk and the counter, from his small enclosure.

I leave what I'm doing and go in.

"Yes, sir?"

"Sit down Claudia."

"You know I'm having Lora Sinclair, well now Lora Wood, to come in next week and start doing some investigating on the old Marian Atchley case. I hope you two can work together on this. Wouldn't it make Daddy proud if we finally solved it?"

"Sure would." I'm smiling and nodding. Underneath, I don't know why he couldn't have just had me work on it. I was there, working for his daddy when the girl disappeared. But I guess it won't hurt to have some fresh eyes on it.

"I know what you're thinking. You think that you could have done this by yourself," he smiles his contagious smile. "And you could. But. I only have one deputy. I need you to keep us all running. Before Lora comes, I want to ask you the details of what you remember about the case and how Dad approached it."

"It's been so long, Will. I'll tell you what I remember and give you all the files on the case."

"Okay, start with the day of the disappearance."

"I was so young, just over 21. We got a call that morning from a frantic mother, who had run more than a mile to get to a phone to report her daughter missing."

"What time was that?"

"We will have to look at those old records, Will. I'm 60 years old. That wasn't yesterday."

"Who took the call?"

"I did. I put it tstraight hrough to Sheriff Jackson. He left immediately for the Curly Willow Creek community."

"Did he take anyone with him?"

"We had a full-time deputy back then. He went too. By the time they got there, folks from the church and neighbors from down the hill were swarming all over the yard. And that little puppy was still there, scared. He was wearing a leash of braided hay strings. The mama said that Marian must have made it for him."

"How long was it from the last time her mother saw her and when she discovered her missing?"

"Again, check the report. But I don't think it was more than 15 minutes."

"Okay. I guess I need you to pull all that paperwork, and we will go out and bring the boxes down so Lora can start working. Claudia, if you think of something that might not be in the reports, you'll let me know, right?"

"Sure thing." I go to the back room and start looking for the old files. The filing cabinets are not in the best place. I can smell the mildew, so I know the ink on those old papers is probably smearing and fading. But I search until I see what I'm looking for and put all the files in a plastic tote.

CHAPTER 16
Lora and Sam

Sam and I go back to our hotel and check out.

"Where to now?" I ask. This is so fun. Only a person like me would think this is the ideal honeymoon. It's all so mysterious and interesting. I don't know that I'm convinced these legends are based on truth, but we haven't finished our tour yet.

Sam is listening to the radio and drumming happily on the steering wheel. He looks over and gives me a wink. My heart jumps.

"Better keep your eyes on the road," I say reaching for his hand.

"Want to fill me in on what you know on the next stop? Is there an expert we can talk to?"

"Which question do you want me to answer

first?"

"How about you fill me in."

So he began the tale.

"We are going to the small town of Flatwoods in Braxton County. On a summer night in 1952 two brothers, Edward and Fred May, and their friend Tommy Hyer were outside when they saw a bright object cross the sky.

It landed on nearby property owned by F. Bailey Fisher. They went home and told their mother, Kathleen May, what they had seen.

"The three boys along with two other local children were accompanied by Mrs. May and a West Virginia National Guardsman Eugene Lemon. They went to investigate.

"Lemon said they saw a pulsing red light. When he aimed a flashlight at it, he saw a 'man-like-figure' with a round red face surrounded by a pointed hood."

"Did they catch it?"

"Just wait Miss Impatient. There is more.

"A noted paranormal investigator described the figure as being about 10 feet tall. Mrs. May said it had claw-like-hands and a head that resembled the ace of spades.

"The local newspaper also reported seeing odd,

gummy skid marks and noted a pungent mist, leading to speculation that it was a UFO landing with an alien in the West Virginia hills.

"Skeptics say that it could have been a light shower that illuminated a barn owl perched in a tree. They say that could have caused the distorted image."

"Did Dr. Cutty have information on this monster?"

"When I talked to her by phone, she did give me some background. It seems that residents' affection for their local folkloric monsters' ties into a growing interest in the paranormal and cryptozoology in popular culture.

"According to Cutty, there is local interest in Flatwoods and in Point Pleasant to form museums and festivals centered around their famous 'monsters.' She says there is already some merchandising going around in those towns."

I stretch and lay my head back on the headrest of the truck.

"Don't get sleepy. We should be there soon."

"Okay. I'm just going to close my eyes for a minute."

When I wake up 30 minutes later, we have reached our destination in Flatwoods.

"I'm afraid there may not be anyone here to talk to," says Sam as we ride around the small downtown.

"I think I'll step inside this little pharmacy and see if someone can give me some direction. Want to come?"

"Sure." I look in the truck mirror and see that I do look like I've been asleep. Oh, well. I run my hand through my hair and hop out to join Sam who is already at the old leaded glass door of the pharmacy.

When I get inside, Sam is talking to the pharmacist, a medium-height distinguished gentleman in his mid-fifties who wears his still-thick light brown hair combed straight back. His beard is meticulously groomed, and he is wearing little round glasses down on the bridge of his nose. The front pocket of his tan smock are stuffed with pens and another pair of glasses.

"I'm Sam Wood. My wife and I are here to do a little research on the Flatwoods Monster legend. I'm a school teacher and hope to incorporate some of this West Virginia lore in my state history class. Can you point me to a local expert?"

"Glad to meet you, Sam. Looks like you have found one of the experts right here. I'm Haskell Porter. Since I don't have any customers right now, why don't you and your wife have a seat on the stools over by the soda fountain. We can talk until I have to do a little business."

I look at Lora and give her a wink. What good luck. We take our seats, and I get out my notebook as Mr. Porter moves to the soda counter.

"Get you something to drink?" he asks.

"Not right now, but for sure before we go."

"Well okay. Better be careful about calling our Green Monster an urban legend around here, son. These people take their monster very seriously."

"I'll watch that, sir. What can you tell me?"

"You know the background, I assume?"

"Oh, yes sir. What is your take on all this?"

"Well, I wasn't living here when this supposedly happened. But as soon as I moved to the area, it became obvious that many folks in these parts really believe. Something must have happened. I'm not sure what.

"Some say it is an alien from a UFO landing. They speculate that since we are up on a ridge, we have a better chance of being a landing spot for alien visitors. And, it didn't look like any monster we have ever heard of or seen concocted in fiction. It was different."

"Don't some think it might have been some kind of bird?" asks Lora.

"Some say perhaps a barn owl."

"Government officials and the Air Force suggest that red light in the sky was a meteor. It's also a possibility that the pulsing red lights were aircraft hazard/navigation beacons. They suggest that the witnesses' stories were exaggerated because of their 'state of anxiety.'"

I notice Lora staring at something on a high shelf behind the counter. There, perched on high, were ceramic representations of the monster. Mr. Porter smiled when he saw that we had noticed them.

"Do you need a Flatwoods monster for your class? I think I can donate one for educational purposes."

We all smile as he reaches for one of the figurines.

"What do *you* think, Mr. Porter?" asks Sam.

"Well, I'll tell you. I think that some of our people believe the legend. Some want to believe it for the notoriety it brings our small community. And some a skeptics and are sick of hearing about it. I think I believe a little of all three theories."

I hear the bell on the pharmacy door jingle as a

customer arrives.

"We better get out of your way," I say, helping Sam gather his things.

"Not before you get something to go. What will it be?"

"Cherry Coke for me, and a milkshake for Sam."

What a nice man. This little adventure hasn't been as scary as I had thought.

CHAPTER 17
Claudia

I've been sitting on the concrete floor of our archives room for two days now trying to find any information on the cold case of missing Marian Atchley that happened in 1959. Unfortunately this storage room is not the ideal place to store important documents.

The concrete floors add to the humidity. I'm doing my best. So far, I have located some files. I wonder if there is anything in them that isn't in the documents found at the church or vice versa.

I have officers' reports and statements from the parents and neighbors. There are even a few photographs taken of the home site and its proximity to where Marian and her puppy were playing.

Thanks to the humidity, and the fact that the

photos were stored front to front, some have stuck together. I have put them out on newspaper on the big legal table to see if they will dry enough that I can peel them a part without too much damage.

I do love Will Jackson, but frankly, I think this is a wild-goose chase. I'd love for us to crack this case, but I'm not too hopeful. I'll keep digging. Here is the photo I was hoping to find. It shows the dog and the collar and leash. I look closely.

It was a flat five-string plait. I know this because my grandparents taught me how to braid or plait. They made primitive pieces that were used around the farm. They did leather repairs on reins and saddles and put cane bottoms in chairs.

By the time I was eight years old, I could do a five-braid plait with hay strings. To keep me busy, my grandmother would hook five strings over a fence post and get me started. I could finish it by myself, but it wasn't the neatest job.

A five-braid is a pretty complex plait for a five-year-old to do by herself. Who helped her? Maybe someone started it, and she finished it.

I doubt Will has ever noticed this. I'm jotting down notes like this for Lora when she starts her investigation. Who in the area did leather work or crafts of this type in this area in 1959? Fat chance of finding that person all these years later. And the possibility of their knowing this child is surely a long shot.

Now, I have to see if I can get up from sitting cross-legged on this floor for such a long time. Tomorrow I'm bringing a cushion.

CHAPTER 18
Sam

Today is day three of our honeymoon and monster hunt in West Virginia. Lora rides beside me in the truck with her nose stuck in a book. She is oblivious to my attempts at conversation and the scenery that is flying by our truck window. If she doesn't stop reading soon, I'll take her book away.

"Hey, you!" I shake Lora's book, and she looks up at me, closes her book, and smiles.

"Sorry, you know how I am once I start reading."

"Nothing you can read is as thrilling as our day is going to be. Do you want to hear about the big daddy of all the monsters? Mothman?"

I make a creepy noise that makes her giggle.

"When I stepped out of our meeting, what did Dr. Cutty tell you about Mothman?"

"We already knew the background story. Witness reports feature an urban legend of several sightings of a winged-humanoid that appeared in the sky and trees in the mid-1960s.

"One sighting was reported by teenagers parking near the site of a secret World War II munitions factory outside of town."

I glance over at Lora, and she is taking all this in, with a serious look on her face.

"Dr. Cutty says the investigation was kicked up a notch when a sighting was reported that coincided with the Silver Bridge disaster. Forty-six people died when the suspension bridge over the Ohio River collapsed in December of 1967.

"Gosh, Sam, how do you remember all these details? We just talked to her."

"I'm pretending you are my class and I'm lecturing."

"Oh, right. I'm hungry. Are you?"

Lora Wood is always hungry. We aren't far from Point Pleasant, so I'll try to convince her to wait until we get into town. We ride a while in silence. Lora is looking through her journal at the notes she took during our visit with Dr. Cutty.

"Sam, Cutty said in our interview, 'This best-known West Virginia legend encompasses history, urban legend, hoaxes, rumors and more.'" I nod in agreement.

"That it does. Let's see what we find."

We pull into Point Pleasant, a small Appalachian town with a population of a little over 4,000. I don't have an expert lined up for this location.

"Let's see if we can find a Chamber of Commerce or some such organization."

And sure enough, we find what we are looking for in a brick and stone building on Main Street.

"Come on, get out and stretch your legs. We can go inside and inquire—if we can't talk now, we can go back later."

I'm expecting to be greeted by an older person who loves his or her job here—talking to visitors about the community and its local lore.

Instead, we find a young woman in her late 20s wearing jeans, lace-up boots, and sporting several piercings in her ears. She greets us with enthusiasm.

"Hi, welcome to Point Pleasant! I'm Abigail Sweeny."

We introduce ourselves and explain our mission in her town—to learn more about the Mothman legend and its continuing presence in the community.

"Oh, I love to talk about the Mothman.

"What's your best description of it?" I ask.

"There are a few living witnesses around. Some are willing to talk about their sightings, and some have never spoken about what they saw. The most common description is a being about seven feet tall, gray in color, with two distinct, red eyes about the size of baseballs.

"Would you like for me to take you on a little tour? We can talk while we ride."

"Sure. Do you have to wait for someone to be here in the office before we can go?"

"Heck no. I just flip the open/closed sign and lock the door. Come on. We can go in my van."

We climb into her five-passenger minivan which is littered with Point Pleasant brochures and maps.

"Help yourself to any of the material on the backseat or on the floor. I'm not the neatest person, but I love my job and my town."

"Where are we going?" asks Lora.

"Some think the Mothman sightings have come as a warning before a disaster. The most famous incident is its appearance before the collapse of the Silver Bridge which killed 46 people. So, first we will drive over the replacement of that bridge.

"Then we will visit the creepy WWII ammo bunkers, where the Mothman was seen. These bunkers were part of the top-secret Virginia Ordnance Works facility. It was an ammo storage and manufacturing plant that was active during WWII." Abigail leans forward in the driver's seat, rummaging around in the scattered literature.

"I thought I had a pamphlet on that. Oh, well."

"Abigail, you speak with certainty that the Mothman existed or exists. No doubt on your part?"

She waits a minute or two before she responds.

"Mr. Wood I haven't seen this creature with my own eyes. The sightings happened before I was born. But I have talked to eye-witnesses. It is clear that they believe the legend to be true. I've seen the impact this lore has had on our community all these years later."

"You don't think all this is for tourist purposes? I'm sure it has been good for the Point Pleasant economy."

"Today, people aren't in fear of the monster. They embrace the legend. And yes, it has been good for the town. There is talk of a festival in the near future. And, I'm not saying it isn't true."

After all this conversation, we are finally at the deserted ammo bunker. We get out, walking over some rough terrain to look at the old bunkers, covered with vines and old signage. The dark sky makes the picture seem even more gloomy.

We are back in Abigail's van and on the way back to town. We have reservation at the historic Lowe Hotel, built in 1901.

She lets us out at our truck and volunteers to help us with any more questions we might have. Lora has filled a whole legal pad with notes. Glad I brought her along for notetaking *and* honeymooning.

We spend the night at the Lowe, which is a little creepy, itself. Maybe it's just because it's old and decorated in vintage furnishings.

After tonight we will head back home and start our new life together. We will probably talk about our discoveries on the ride back, but I'm ready to put this haunting business on hold until I can transcribe it for my lecture notes.

I'm ready to pay some attention to my bride.

CHAPTER 19
Claudia

This is my last day to be checking out material to reopen the Atchley case. Lora Sinclair, now Wood, will be coming Monday. Will says I need to help her.

I guess I've already made my mind up to think I know more than she does. After all, I'm the one with the law enforcement training. I have been here for a long time and am familiar with the case.

Maybe I'm being unfair. She is young and college-educated. Maybe a fresh set of eyes on all this documentation will be good. I'll guess I'll have to give her a chance. I may have to swallow my pride and hope for a team effort in solving this case.

Will hasn't been able to locate the Atchleys, Marian's parents. I'm not sure they are still alive. I wonder what I'd do if my precious daughter disappeared. Would I stay in the area and continue to hope, or would I do like they did and relocate?

I'm going to see if I can find something on them in the police database. I know Will has looked before, but technology has changed so much in the last few years, maybe I can find a hint.

To get us off on the right foot, I'm going to call Lora tomorrow and fill her in on what I'm doing and tell her I'm ready to go to work whenever she is.

CHAPTER 20
Lora

There were still a few days of spring break left when we got home. We had planned to fish off the deck, hike to some new places that I hadn't seen, and just get used to being married. Even though it was March, it rained every day for the rest of the week. It was a cold, mountain rain, sometimes mixed with bits of ice—just enough to make you slip when you turned the corner on the stone sidewalk of the cabin. The pine needles were encapsulated in ice, making them look like tiny ornaments.

There were good times too during this first winter as a couple. We talked late into the night and slept until we wanted to get up. Married love was so much more relaxed and sweeter. I knew that I'd make the right choice in a mate.

Our bedroom was just big enough for us to

walk around the bed. There was a dresser in the main living space of the cabin. A small nook with an old tablecloth hanging over the opening served as a closet. Where was I going to put my things? The bathroom held a clawfoot tub with a circular shower curtain contraption, and the sink was a tiny galvanized tub crammed in one corner of the room.

I didn't want to complain about space because I knew Sam would think I was pushing him to move into Helen's beautiful cabin. I took him there and told him about her offer, and it scared him to death.

So I'm waiting for him to bring the subject up again. He may get sick of having me under foot all the time.

Sam had the idea to make a drawer on wheels that could roll under the bed for our shoe and boot storage. He knew we were cramped. We had more ideas about storage. We made rough book selves to hold my books and other treasures. I added a piece or two to the mantle. Before I came, mantle décor consisted of a gun and a couple of empty beer cans.

Since Sam is an artist, one of his carvings—a hawk with wings spread wide—soared above the rough hewn mantle. The bird's minute features and feathers were captured beautifully in the wood. The almost life-size carving of me with my arm around

Goose sits near the kitchen screen door as if we are looking at the lake.

We also began learning each other's likes and dislikes. I tried a few typically Southern dishes on him—cabbage, onions and bacon browned in an old iron skillet; butter beans; and iced tea with meals. It's growing on him. I think mountain people usually drink hot tea or coffee. When I asked for iced tea at the store one day, Mrs. Josie, Rex's mama, looked at me like I had asked for a straight shot of whiskey.

In return she gave me some West Virginia recipes to try on Sam. These were some of the dishes she told me about when I first met her and interviewed her about the culture of the mountain people. Sam perked up when I tried dishes with ramps, an onion-like plant. He laughed at my version of a peperoni roll. Folks in this state eat a lot of venison, as do Mississippians.

So we compromised and decided what worked best for us. The other day, I think I heard Sam say "y'all."

When we weren't building storage solutions and cooking, Sam worked on his syllabus for the history class to include the monster lore. I can't wait to see what his students already knew about these legends and what they do and do not believe.

By Sunday afternoon we knew we needed to get out of the cabin for fresh air no matter what the weather looked like. After a lunch of stew and cornbread, something we both liked, we decided we were coming down with cabin fever and put on our rain gear, coats, and boots and headed outside to let Goose run. He always stays with us.

After days of being inside and only going out for his business breaks, Goose was running wildly, his nose to the ground. We sat down on a nice outcropping of rock to catch our breath. We sat there, breathing hard, our faces and noses red from the cold. My hair had come partially down from its braid and was sticking to my wet cheeks.

"We did the right thing, didn't we Lora Madison Sinclair Wood?"

"Yes, we did….." My answer was smothered out by a warm, steamy kiss.

"We better find Goose and head back," said Sam, who had picked up a long stick and stripped the twiggs off to make a walking stick.

I looked to the West and could see the orange of sunset beginning to glow against the mountains.

"If I see orange, that means sun is somewhere," I said. "Maybe tomorrow we will see sunlight."

"Yep, maybe sun tomorrow. Goose!! Here boy."

There was no rustle in the leaves, no barking, no nothing. Goose hardly ever gets too far out of our sight. He usually runs ahead of us, the comes bounding back as if to say, "Y'all sure are slow. Come on!"

I called; Sam whistled. Thirty minutes went by and it was getting darker.

"We aren't far from the cabin. Let's head that way. I'll get in the truck and ride down the road a little later. I'm sure he got the scent of a squirrel or a female dog in heat. Don't worry. He'll come back."

We ate a little leftover cornbread and soup and a piece of apple pie that Mrs. Josie had sent us, but it was hard to get anything down.

Sam finally pushed his chair back and put on his coat. "I'm going to take one more drive before we turn in."

He stayed gone about an hour. When he came in the door, by the look of him I knew he had not found his dog.

Sleep came hard that night. We lay in our snug bed, curled against each other and listened for every sound—the breaking of a stick or a distant animal sound. Sam got up several times, and I heard him open the door hoping to hear the sound of Goose's tail thumping on the wooden porch.

The next morning was Monday and no Goose. Sam had to go back to school, and I was to start my research job with the sheriff. The search will have to wait until we get back home this afternoon.

CHAPTER 21
Claudia/Lora

I got to the office today about 7. I wanted to make sure I had all my material together and ready to reopen the Atchley case. Will is interested in all this and wants it checked out, but he has other things on his mind. Drug cases. These mountains are full of them.

At 7:15 I fired up the computers, made coffee, said a prayer that I would keep my smart mouth shut and be nice to this young woman—all for the sake of bringing closure to this cold case of Marian Atchley.

I had just downed my second sip of coffee when the door opened, and Lora Wood entered. She was not pretentious or overly-dressed. Good thing because we may be sitting on the concrete floor of the file room again. She wears her long hair braided over one shoulder. Her outfit of jeans, hiking boots, and a long sweater over a t-shirt say a lot about her. I may like her after all.

"Hello, Mrs. Claudia," she says as she approaches my desk and drops a big tote bag down in the wooden chair across from me.

"Hi, Lora. Just call me Claudia. Are you ready to go to work?"

"Yes, ma'am. Where should I start?"

"I guess we better wait for Sheriff Jackson to get here and give us some orders. I've been pulling documents from the files for you to go over. I think the plan is for us to go to the church where we can spread out and not be disturbed."

"Sounds great," says Lora. "Do I need to start putting those things in my truck? I dropped Sam off at school today so I could have the truck."

"Will, I mean Sheriff Jackson, will probably let us take the department's Bronco. Come with me to the file room, and I'll show you what we have."

"Have you known the sheriff long, Claudia?"

"I started working here for Will's daddy, Sheriff Frank Jackson, in 1959. That was the same year that this little girl went missing."

"You remember details?"

"I do, some. I know Frank Jackson didn't run for reelection because this unsolved case got under his skin so bad. We can talk more about that when we get set up at the church."

I unlocked the file room door and showed Lora the big plastic box that contained the department's files. There were clippings from several newspapers in two cardboard file boxes, also stacked against one wall.

Lora opened her mouth to ask another question, and we heard the bell on the front door ring. By the sound of the footsteps, big man in cowboy boots, I knew the sheriff was in.

"We are in here, Will," I called out. He popped his head in the door and spoke to us both. "Lora, can I see you in about five minutes in my office?"

"Sure," she said. She waited until she heard Will pour a cup of coffee and sit down in his desk chair, a big, worn, brown leather chair that made a horrible squeak every time he leaned back. She went in.

"Lora, welcome. Do you remember exactly what we talked about when I asked you to do some organizational research on this case?"

"Yes, has anything changed?"

"We sent the scrap of fabric off to the state crime lab. It's back. It was identified as human blood.

We are using a forensic process known as DNA profiling. We need something from the original files that we can test for a match. If you run across any hair or cloth, that's what I'm looking for.

"Come on, I'll help you and Claudia get the boxes in the Bronco. Then you can go up to the church and set up your temporary headquarters. Here's the key." He started to walk away.

"Oh, Claudia may give you a little trouble at first, but she will come around. I don't know what I'd do without her. She's a good fit for this department. She just might be a little jealous. Got it?"

"Got it. Oh, Sheriff Jackson? If you or the other deputy are up around Sam's cabin on patrol, could you be on the lookout for our black lab, Goose? He just disappeared out of nowhere yesterday afternoon. Totally not like him to get far from us. It's a bad way to start off our marriage." I stopped just before a tear crept into the corner of my eye. I hope he missed it.

"Sure thing. Black Lab? Collar?"

"Yes, he has a red collar and vet tag."

He gave me a thumbs up and strode off in the direction of the file room.

After loading the Bronco, Claudia and I head up the narrow, curvy road to the church. The scenery is breathtaking. On the way, Claudia gives me the background of the case again, adding a few details.

"You know something?" Claudia said. "I've looked at all this stuff several times over the years. I noticed something when I was getting this box ready that I'd never seen before."

"Oh, what was it?" I turned my head back to her and away from the mountains and greenery whizzing by.

"In that photo of the puppy with his leash, I noticed that it was a slip collar that was braided in a five-strand flat braid. That's pretty complex for a little girl."

"How did you know what it was?"

"My granddaddy did a little leather work. Nothing fancy. He fixed a few bridles, punched a few holes, and braided some reins. My grandmother taught me to do a five-plait. I guess I was about eight years old when I finally got the hang of it. This little girl was younger than that."

"Good point! Who else would have done leather work in this area in that time period?"

"Nobody I know. Think we should look into it?"

"Absolutely! We can ask around." said Lora. I knew Claudia was proud of herself for finding this new lead, and she should be. Maybe this will help ease any tension between us.

We park the vehicle and walk up the steps to the church. I could tell that it has once been beautiful—not especially ornate—but in a spectacular setting that let churchgoers look down over the mountain at all below. Once, made of white board siding, the church had been bricked at some point with a stone foundation and steps.

Claudia inserted the key in the lock and the door creaked on its hinges as it opened. I was immediately struck with the smell of old building—dampness, maybe a little mold, and a mustiness that comes from being closed up with no ventilation. Maybe if the workers can get back on the job, they can take care of that.

I could see that a little wing off the sanctuary had been cleared for us. It had a sliding partition that could be closed and made the area useful as a Sunday School room or whatever was needed.

We spent the next few hours sorting the material. The time flew as we made piles of clippings, documents, and photos on one table. On another set up parallel to the first, we did the same with the material that was found at the church.

Claudia has brought pimiento cheese sandwiches and chips for our lunch. It was good to stop and take a break.

After lunch, we started the task of going through the material. I took one table; Claudia took the other. We made a list of contents in each pile.

It took me a couple of hours to go through the document file. There was so much there. Claudia had chosen to go through the church material because she was familiar with what came through the Sheriff's Office. She had not seen the information in the church boxes and was likely to notice new information.

"Claudia, who would have had access to the church that could have stored all this material in the window seats?"

"Will and I have gone over this, as did Frank Jackson. As far as we could tell, the pastor, church secretary, custodian, and really just about anyone from deacons to Sunday School teachers could have gone up there without anyone thinking anything about it."

"Were those people questioned?"

"It should be in the documents pile that you have. Might be in a separate folder."

There was so much to consider. Obvious angles were thoroughly investigated by Frank Jackson and his team in 1959. I was looking for a new lead.

We wrapped up about 4 o'clock and after locking up the church, made our way back to town. I was excited and couldn't wait to tell Sam all about my day. While we were working, I would forget about Goose for a minute or two. When I remembered, a knot in my stomach lurches.

The damper on everything was our missing Goose. Where could that dog be?

CHAPTER 22
Sam

I got home today before Lora. The first thing I did was put on my hiking gear and head out, looking for my dog. There are not many people traveling this road. I've thought of every scenario—someone picked him up, he got hit by a car or shot, he chased a critter or another dog off and got turned around. None of those sound reasonable for Goose.

Last night I drove the roads and saw no indication that he had been hit. As to the "got lost" theory, as much as we have walked these trails in the woods, he knew how to find his way home. In fact, sometimes he knew his way when I didn't.

Today in better light, I'm looking for more details like a newly-broken branch, dog poop, paw prints, blood, anything that could be a clue. I brought my whistle with me.

As sad as facing the possibility that I'd lost my dog was, I couldn't imagine losing a child like this with no closure, no answer. I thought about little Marian Atchley and the case Lora was helping with. Would I stay in the area or put all the heartache behind me and relocate? The Atchleys must have chosen to relocate. The sheriff says they have been unable to trace them after 1964.

Bringing my mind back to concentrate on my own hunt, I called and whistled. Every time I did, I expected the foliage to part and to see Goose running full throttle toward me with his tongue hanging out of his mouth sideways. But there was nothing. I hunted until almost dark. Finally I heard the sound of the iron dinner bell that hangs on my porch. Lora must be home and worried about me.

Guess it's time to call it quits for the day. Up ahead I heard a rustling in the undergrowth and froze. Listening intently, I finally saw a porcupine waddling across the trail. When it saw or smelled me, he waddled a little faster.

On the way back to the cabin, I reviewed my day at school. At least that was something good. Kids are always restless after a break. Some are glad to be back at school and to have some organization in their lives. Some are like worms in hot fire.

I have to remind myself that my seventh-grade kids come from all different backgrounds—from families that nurture their children and provide for them to those who come to school wearing the same clothes for days. Their faces are dirty and their hair uncombed. I suspect they get up by themselves and get to school the best way they can. Some parents are addicts, many are just living in terrible poverty.

When I came in to history today we reviewed the material where we left off. I could tell that by the end of the period, I was losing them.

"Hey guys, let's stop right here, and we will pick it back up tomorrow. We have about 15 minutes left. Let's have some discussion." I could feel their eyes rolling at the mere mention of discussion.

"You know in our study of West Virginia there is a topic I thought you might like. Have any of you heard that some people here believe that we live in one of the most haunted states? Tell me what you know about our ghosts and monsters."

The room had gotten quiet and there was no wiggling and squirming.

"Anyone?"

A boy in the second seat from the front row makes eye contact with me. He is usually shy and hesitant to speak in class. I notice he wears the same flannel shirt each day over different T-shirts. I'm thinking he doesn't have a coat.

"Albert, did you want to say something."

The boy looks down at his desk and then back at me.

"My grandma used to tell me there were ghosts down by the creek."

"Oh, really. What did you think about that?"

"I just didn't go to the creek."

"Have any of you heard of The Mothman, or Braxie, the Green Monster, or any others?"

A few kids raised their hands.

"Is this something you would like to talk about in the next few weeks, the legends, the lore, possible explanations for the stories? Stuff like that."

Almost the whole class nodded. Bingo, I had them back.

"Okay then. Ask around at home and see what your family thinks about this subject, and then write down a few notes. I'll grade your responses as a daily grade. We will start on this probably week after next."

The bell rang, and they were gone. Except for Randi. She stopped by my desk and said, "Mr. Wood, I don't believe in ghosts and monsters." She looked down while she was talking.

"That's okay, Randi. I'm not asking you to believe in ghosts and monsters. We are going to talk about how these stories started, how they were handed down from one generation to the other.

"Do you remember Albert saying that his grandmother told him there were ghosts by the creek?"

"Yes, sir," she said, finally rising her eyes to meet mine.

"Do you think maybe that story started to keep the kids from going down to the creek alone where they might get hurt or get in water too deep?"

"Maybe," she said. "I just don't want to get scared talking about this stuff."

"I promise I will try to make it fun, and at the same time teach you all more about West Virginia's history. How does that sound?"

I saw a slight smile cross her lips. She looked up and nodded.

"Okay then, deal?"

"Deal!" she said.

"Run on, you'll be late for your next class."

Randi turned and gave me a little wave before she left the room. You never know how kids will react to something.

CHAPTER 23
Buck
Sinclair Farm, Mississippi

Simsie went to the doctor today, and she confirmed that she was pregnant! Looks like we might have a baby in November or early December. We are so excited. I think maybe we are too excited since it's so early. Simsie came in the door all smiles. Her auburn hair was hanging loose around her shoulders, and the few freckles that were dotted on her nose were shining. I can't believe this beautiful girl is my wife.

Her hands were full of brochures about being pregnant, booklets about childbirth and infant care, and a big bottle of pre-natal vitamins that were as big as some cow pills I've seen. I don't see how she can swallow one of those things.

She plopped down on the couch, and we went over how much the doctor would charge for her services, and how much the hospital bill could be. It's a good thing we have insurance through Simsie's work. Still, we need to be saving all we can.

This is a big drafty old house. I may have to ask Lora if we can add some insulation to our room. The big bedroom has plenty of space for a crib, so the baby can sleep there until it's older.

I talk to Lora a good bit this time of year. Early spring calves have come and are doing great. Some of the equipment we have is getting older. I'm glad that Mr. Asa taught me how to fix it and keep it running. Those new big tractors scare me a little.

Guess I need to start planning for replacement of our main tractor in a few years. You can't save enough money for an expense that big. I'm sure that we will have to borrow money when the time comes.

Since Simsie and I moved in the farm house right after we got married, we have tried to make some kind of small improvement each month. We have painted the beadboard in hall a light tan. It had very dark, floral wall paper on it that was peeling. Now it is lighter and leads you right into the dining room at the end.

We replaced the old wooden windows across

the whole back of the dining room. Simsie hated to do away with anything original to the house, but the windows rattled every time the wind blew. The room was always cold in winter and hard to cool in the summer. In the end, it was a good decision.

There is so much to do, but we have only been here three months. Next project will be replacing rotten boards around the roof.

Maybe Lora will come visit soon. By then I hope she can see a big difference. She should see a big difference in Simsie, too. By then, we will know what kind of baby we are having. Life is good.

CHAPTER 24
Lora

Day two of our research had gotten off to a late start. There was a big truck accident on the highway that demanded the attention of Sheriff Jackson and the Deputy Coleman. That left Claudia in the office answering calls and relaying information on the radio.

The truck was carrying hazardous material which had spilled onto the road, and that made the accident more difficult. When I got to the office, Claudia was busy communicating with fire department officials on proper procedure for processing the scene and when nearby residents might be in danger.

She finally got a break. "Would you be uncomfortable going to the church to work alone?

This situation may take hours to resolve."

"No, I'll be fine. Want me to go on up there?"

Claudia, now back on the phone, handed me the key and nodded. So off I went.

At least it was a pretty, sunny day. When we were here yesterday, it was raining and gloomy. The church was giving off a musty, old building smell. I hope the dampness and humidity hadn't damaged any of the material found upstairs.

I looked over my notes. Scrolling through the list of contacts that Claudia had compiled for me, I found the number for the Methodist preacher who holds services there on Sunday. Since our investigation started, the congregation has agreed to use the sanctuary only and not disturb our material in the partitioned side room.

I dialed the number for Rev. Simon Watson, who lives in a small community about five miles from the church.

He answered on the third ring.

"Rev. Watson?"

"Yes."

It took me a minute to recover my surprise at talking to a very young man. I had expected to find an older man who might be spending his retirement years leading this low-key, part-time church.

"Hi, my name is Lora Wood. I'm working with the sheriff's department in investigating the Atchley case and the material found in your church. Do you have a minute to talk?"

"Absolutely. In fact, I was just thinking about coming to the church to pick up a legal pad that I made notes on for this coming Sunday's message. Would it be okay for us to talk in person?"

"Oh, yes. That would be great. I do have several questions."

"Okay, I'll see you in about 20 minutes."

"Great. See you then."

What good fortune. I usually do better talking to people in person than I do on the phone. You can read body language and sense emotions better one-on-one. I still am not sure what has qualified me for this case. I hope my interviewing skills will be close to what is needed for law enforcement questioning.

A few minutes later, the front door opens and a young man in medical scrubs walks in. He has sandy brown hair and a full, neatly-trimmed beard.

"Bet you were expecting me to be older," he says, smiling.

I stood to greet him. "Well, to be truthful, yes. Let's go back here where I'm working and sit down.

"I see you must have a second job in the medical

field."

"You don't think I can live on the $75 a week that I make here, do you? I just finished nursing school and am working at the local hospital in ICU. My wife teaches high school."

"Oh really, maybe she knows my husband, Sam Wood?"

"Oh, yes. I've heard her mention him. He's the most popular teacher there, according to her. All the little girls have a crush on him."

"Maybe I better take his lunch to him at school one day, so they know he's taken."

"Rev. Watson, I know you are busy, but I do have some questions. In a way, I do wish you were older so you might remember some of the history of other congregations who met here and people who might have had access to the church during that time—1959."

"I'm afraid I can't help you much there. We do have a list of past congregations and pastors that I can share with you. As to who could have gone up in the tower and stored a box there, that would be harder to pin down. We did have full-time services here for years. There were secretaries and church personnel that would fall into that category."

"Are any of those pastors from that time period

still living?"

"Let me get that list for you. Is the copier on? I'll copy what I have."

He goes into the back office and emerges with an old-fashioned, black ledger.

"Here you go, copy whatever you need from this book. It's old, so just handle with care. Unfortunately, I have a shift in about an hour, so I will have to go. Good luck with all this, and please call me if you have more questions."

"Thanks Rev. Watson."

"Oh, Simon, please. And I'll tell my wife we made the school connection for her and Sam."

After he leaves, I look around the church and the piles of documents and photos, and the ledger, and the task seems insurmountable. I will sit down with the ledger and make some notes and copies to get me started.

I straightened up my work, took one last look around the church, locked all the doors, and began my drive back to town. I can't wait to get home to see Sam. Maybe there will be enough light to go look again for Goose.

Sam is trying to be interested in my work and

starting a routine for our marriage, but I can see the sadness in his eyes. I love that goofy dog so much. I have to remind myself that he was Sam's dog before I ever came along.

When I get to the cabin and walk in, Sam is on the phone with his friend Rex. I hear his end of the conversation.

"Hey, man. Got some bad news. Goose has been missing for three days now. I don't guess you have seen anything of him……..Do you know anyone who has a tracking dog? Maybe one used for rescue?……..Oh, yeah? Wait, let me get a pen and something to write on."

He scrambles in his book bag and pulls out pen and paper.

"Okay, go ahead………Silas Parsons……. bloodhound……address and phone number?"

He makes more notes.

"Great. I think I'll give him a call. Things going alright with you and your mama?…….Good deal. Thanks, buddy."

He hangs up and comes over to give me a long hug and a kiss.

"Did Rex have a contact?"

"He did. I think I'll give this guy a call. He lives about two miles from here. A good dog might be able to pick up Goose's scent. How was your day?"

I go over the meeting with the pastor and my organizing the documents, which, so far, has led to nothing.

"While you get settled, I'm going to call this guy. We are expecting more rain over the next few days."

"Mr. Parsons? My name is Sam Wood. My friend Rex tells me that you have a pretty good search and rescue dog."

"Yessir, Mr. Wood, I do. Name's Silas. What or who are you searching for?"

"My black lab disappeared about three days ago. No sign of him. My wife and I have searched the woods near our house, roads, everywhere he could be and no luck. Would you be willing to let your dog take a run and see if he picks up his scent? I'll be glad to pay you whatever your fee is. I teach school and get home every day about 3:45."

"Be glad to, Sam. The sooner the better. What about tomorrow afternoon?"

"Great. Hope we haven't waited too long."

"Oh, no," says Mr. Parsons. "Bloodhounds can pick up a scent longer than most search and rescue dogs like shepherds. We have rain moving in tomorrow night, so it would be better to go in the afternoon."

"I think, according to Rex, that I live not far from you."

For the first time since Goose went missing, I see a little spark of hope in Sam's eyes.

CHAPTER 25
Silas Parsons

I'm meeting Sam Wood today to see if my dog can find his dog. Bloodhounds are good, but we have had so much rain that I'm a little doubtful about ole Chief picking up a scent. He's a good dog, still in his prime.

He has been trained and certified in SAR (Search and Rescue) and MAS (Missing Animal Search). My dog is the only one with this certification, that I know of, in this part of the state.

There are so many different jobs that dogs do in Search and Rescue—tracking, trailing, and cadaver locating. Tracking dogs work with their noses to the ground, following human scent, while detection dogs are used in searching for objects, or in the case of police work, drugs. Air scent dogs sniff the air for human smells.

Different dog breeds are used in SAR, but I'm a fan of bloodhounds. I've had some kind of hound since I was a kid. I've had them so long, I don't even mind their hound dog smell anymore, and that's saying a lot. Maybe that's why I don't have a girl-friend right now.

I named this current dog Chief for a reason. He reminded me of an elderly gentleman—retired Fire Chief Homer Sanders—who hangs out at Mrs. Jolie's store in town. I have never heard anyone call him by his first name, just Chief.

Old men love to hang out in the back corners of stores. They talk politics, weather, and love to talk about their dogs and horses most of all.

There is another reason that his name is Chief. My daddy always told me a dog's name should be short and one syllable. Commands and names should be short, to be hollered loudly and quickly.

I go to the back yard and get Chief and wipe the slobber off his mouth and brush the mud off his belly. Those stinky, long ears are a big part of the bloodhound's conformation that make him so good at what he does. The ears flap the scent back up to the dog's nose which has more scent sensors than any other breed.

I snap on his reflective vest and his working

collar which has ID and rabies tags on it. When that final snap clicks, he knows he's ready to go to work. When I take the vest off, he excels at his other job in life, which is lying on the porch and sleeping at my feet. Good dog, Chief.

Off we go, to Sam's cabin. He was right. It is not far from my place. Chief knows we are on a mission. He rides beside me in the front seat. The closer we get, the more he stands up in the seat and pants heavily.

"It's okay, Buddy. You ready to go to work?"

He snaps his mouth shut to get a good breath before dropping a blob of slobber as big as a tea bag on the truck seat. That's why I carry paper towels in the back seat of the truck.

We pull up at Sam's cabin. I must have passed here at least three or four times a week and never noticed the cabin. The driveway looks like it would take you to a field trail but not to a residence.

This must be Sam coming out to meet me.

"Hey, Sam. I'm Silas," I say through the rolled-down window. Sam looks younger than I am, but not by much.

"Come on over the porch," he says. "I have some things for you and Chief to look at."

I leave Chief in the truck with the windows

down, so he won't freak out. Sam shows me several pictures of Goose. He's just a good-looking black lab, no markings, nothing remarkable.

"I brought a blanket from his bed and an old collar that he doesn't wear anymore, but it should still have his scent on it."

"Before I turn him loose, I need to ask you to stay back here. I will follow, but not too closely. He will hunt or search without barking. When he finds his target, he will bark or report. Got it? Show me which direction we are heading?"

Sam points back behind the cabin. "There's an old road bed back there. We had gone about a mile when we lost him."

I bend over and let Chief get a good smell of the collar and the dog blanket. "Search," I tell him and unclip his lead.

Chief is off and running.

He works hard for about an hour, his nose to the ground, his tongue hanging out. Another hour passes with no results. I know he is tired. I decide to call it a day. We wait until Sam catches up with us.

"I think we better quit for today." I can tell Sam is disappointed, but he understands.

"Want to try again tomorrow?" he asks. "I get out of school tomorrow sooner than I did today. We could get an earlier start. What about 2:30?"

"Sounds good. Don't give up, Sam. Sometimes it takes several trips."

Chief and I get here at Sam's cabin at 2 to get ready for the search. We go through the same routine. I will wait until Sam is here and ready before I snap on Chief's vest to signal it's time to go to work.

At 2:30 on the dot, Sam pulls up. "Hey, man. Ready to go to work?"

"You bet," I answer. I notice that Sam is respectful of his behavior around Chief. He doesn't talk to him, pet him, or look him directly in the eye. Most people do that, and I have to nicely tell them that will distract Chief in his hunt.

I reintroduce the scent items to Chief, snap on his vest, and we are off. Sam is hanging back and Chief and I are working ahead. He keeps his nose to the ground, his long ears gathering scent along with mud and other debris.

We started where we left off yesterday.

Turning down the muddy path, we approach a road that looks like nothing more than a cow trail. It looks like an old trail with banks rising on both sides. The erosion of soil on the banks, lets the trees grow out at strange angles.

I follow Chief as he walks slower down the path. Ahead of us is a shack. It looks like no one has lived here for decades. The roof is caving in, and the grass is so tall it has fallen over with the winter freeze.

Chief stops by the shack. He sits and barks. And then he looks back at me.

I tentatively approach the shack. Inside there is no sign of human inhabitants. Then I see an old cooking pot, the handle rusted or broken off long ago. In it were a few pieces of some kind of scraps.

Then I hear a scratching. Looking inside the next so-called room, I see something black in the shadows.

"Goose?" I say. Hard to believe it might be him. Then I hear the thumping of his tail on the floor.

I take the walkie talkie out of my belt holster. It won't work over long distances, but I'm betting Sam is not far behind me.

"Hey Sam, you better go get your truck or a four-wheeler. I found your dog."

Chief sits obediently until I reach out and give him his reward which is a vigorous hug and scratches behind the ears. Then he plops down on the floor, still trying to catch his breath. "Good boy, Chief. Good boy."

CHAPTER 26
Sam

I can't believe Goose is still alive. Silas didn't tell me much except the location of the shack and that the dog was alive. He must be in bad shape since he told me to come in a vehicle.

While alternately running and walking back home, I am reminded how stressful and emotional this whole ordeal has been. And then I think about Marian Atchley's parents and how devastated they must have been. They lost a daughter, never found her, or had closure as to what had happened. I do hope Lora can be a part in solving that mystery.

I get back to the cabin stopping every now and then to breathe. I must have walked about two miles when I got the notice to turn around. I run in the cabin long enough to call Lora at the church where she is working.

"Hey, baby, can you leave for a while? This guy with the dog says he has found Goose. I'm going to drive as far as I can and then I'll walk the rest of the way. He may need to go to the vet."

"Oh, Sam, where was he? Is he hurt? Who…?"

"Don't know any more. Gotta go. Just come home if you can. Or you could meet me at the vet."

"Okay. We are almost through today anyway. Meet you there.

I hang up before she finishes talking. She will understand my hurry. On the way out I grab a small tarp in case we have to carry him."

I drive to the point on the old road where the path leads to the shack. Silas had tied his handkerchief on a pine tree to mark the spot. Grabbling the tarp from the back of the truck, I head down the path. Silas meets me half way.

"He's in pretty rough shape, Sam. Looks like he has in there for about three days, judging from the poop there. He hasn't had much to eat. I gave him some water, a little at a time. Also, looks like he did battle with a porcupine. He has a nose and mouth full of quills that are beginning to get infected."

We get to the shack and I slowly approach Goose who is curled up in the corner. "Hey, Goose, hey boy, you'll be okay." He thumps his tail at the sound of my voice.

I can see the quills. If he'd had food, he couldn't have eaten. He looks thin and scared.

"Do you know who owns this land, Silas?"

"No, but we can find out."

"Now Sam, I don't necessarily see abuse here. I see a dog who is full of quills, infection setting in, not much food. He may have just holed up in here because he was so weak."

Nodding, I don't take my eyes off my dog. I reach my hand out, and he licks my fingers. That's a good sign.

I call Goose over to me, and he puts his head in my lap. He is shaking all over. Probably from pain and weakness. How can a perfectly healthy dog go from the picture of health to this in just a matter of days?

I try to see if he is able to walk to my truck, and it looks like if we go slowly, he can. I load him carefully in the back seat. Silas climbs in the passenger seat, and Chief jumps in the bed of the truck.

'What about the scrap pan? Someone fed him something," I ask Silas as we drive back to town.

"Who knows? May have been a kid that found him and didn't know what to do. Let's see what the vet says."

When I get to the veterinarian's office, Lora comes running out to see the dog. She has a blanket and wraps it around him. "Oh, Goose," she whispers. I already called ahead and told them we were bringing him in."

Our local vet is Dr. Mitchell Granger, a gentleman in his late 60s. His office is in a small two-bedroom house that has served as his headquarters since he moved here in the 1970s. He is more of the old-school type practitioner, but a top-notch doc, in my opinion. His staff consists of his office manager/occasional assistant Judith Cole, a high school kid who comes in on weekends to clean and feed animals, and himself.

Lora and I carefully unload Goose from the back seat. Judith sees us struggling and comes to help.

"Oh, man. What in the world happened to this guy besides a porcupine encounter?"

"We aren't sure," says Lora.

"Can he walk?"

"I think so," I say. "He walked to the truck after

we found him.

"We were about to close, so let's get him right back to the exam room. Dr. Mitch is waiting."

When the vet walks in, I see by his expression that he is concerned about Goose's condition. He helps me get him up on the exam table. Since the room is small, Lora waits by the front desk.

"Well, Sam, there's not much I can tell you that you don't already know. We need to sedate him and get these quills out. The wounds are beginning to get infected, so we need to start him on an antibiotic. He is dehydrated and hungry, so I'll start a slow IV drip to get some fluid back into him. Maybe tomorrow we can start giving him a little food.

"He needs to stay overnight, and tomorrow I can feed him just a little every other hour to get him eating again. I can't give him too much at a time until I see how he's going to tolerate it."

"Do you think he will make a full recovery?" I ask, my hand resting on Goose's head. He is still shaking so hard.

"Oh, yeah, he should. The only problem is that he needs to eat, and after we remove those quills his mouth is going to be pretty sore." Dr. Mitch lifts the dog's lip so that I can see that he has quills inside his mouth as well as in his nose.

"Let's get him sedated. Why don't you stay here with him while I do this? I might need an extra hand. You can tell me more about his situation and how you found him. Did Silas and Chief help you locate him?"

I start to recount the whole story as I watch Goose drift off to sleep.

CHAPTER 27
Lora

Sam told me what Dr. Mitch said about Goose. I don't mind waiting out here by the front desk. It will give me time to calm down. I'm shaking about as hard as Goose is.

"Would you like something to drink while you wait?" asks Judith.

"No, I'm fine, thanks. It's after 5, shouldn't you be off duty?"

"I locked the front door, but I'm staying here with you 'til Goose wakes up from his procedure. If he had a lot of quills, it could be about an hour."

Judith is in her mid-forties, I'd guess. She has reddish, brown hair that just touches her shoulders. When she smiles, her nose crinkles just a bit.

"I like your name. It's old fashioned and

beautiful."

She laughs. "I've been told that before. Actually, I was adopted. I think my adoptive parents changed my name. Judith seems like it's been my name all along."

"Oh, I didn't mean to ask a nosey question."

"Thanks alright. No harm."

I glance at my watch. Judith notices.

"They should be out in about 30 minutes. I know how it is to love a dog. I had a shepherd when I was a little girl. He came with me when I was adopted. He had an original name—Shep." She smiles. "He lived until he was about 12, which is pretty long for a big dog. I loved him so much."

We talked more, but I wasn't listening to much. My mind was racing—reddish hair, mid-40s, shepherd dog, adopted. Was I dreaming? Was it a coincidence? I don't think I asked her prying questions about her past. This is ordinary convrsation to have with someone you've just met. Right?

I decided not to push her any more, but I was already thinking of questions I *wanted* to ask her. I'm sure I'll be back at the vet several times while Goose is healing.

Sam comes out with a stainless steel pan full of

porcupine quills and bloody water.

"Oh, Sam! Did you have to show me that?"

"I wanted you to see why he will be so sore. Doc even had to take a few stitches inside his mouth to get to the really bad ones."

Judith smiles at me.

"I guess you are used to this?"

"I don't get squeamish anymore, but I never get over the feeling of sadness when an animal has been mistreated or is sick and hurting."

I like her, I think to myself. We could be friends. I hope I don't mess that up if it turns out that she is who we are looking for. No telling how she will feel about her past. She probably believes the story she was told all those years ago. But there I go again, assuming I've got an answer.

"Can we go home, Sam?"

"Sure, do you want to come back and say goodnight to Goose?"

"No, I want him to rest so he can get better. I'll see him tomorrow. Dr. Mitch comes out of the back, drying his hands.

"You've got a tough boy there," he says. "I think by the time we get him eating and drinking, he will be able to go home."

After saying goodbye to Judith, I turn and look at

Sam. "I'll see you at home."

"Sure, I'm right behind you. Be careful."

As I drive up the narrow roads to our mountain cabin, I think about what I will tell Sheriff Will Jackson. Will he think I'm jumping the gun? I didn't go looking for this. I just stumbled across it. Who knows? If we confront her in an easy-going manner, we may find something that will rule out her being a grown-up Marian Atchley.

CHAPTER 28
Lora

The next day, I drive down to the vet's office. Judith greets me when I come in the door.

"Morning Lora. I think you'll like what you find back there?"

"I can't wait. Can I see him?"

"Yes. I'll take you back. Doc is doing a little surgery."

"Do you help him when he's in surgery?"

"Sometimes when it is a long one. We just flip the open/closed sign and lock the door. I don't know how much I help. Since I'm not a trained veterinary technician I can't do some things.

"I've thought about going back to college, but at my age—45—it may be too late."

"Oh no. Never too late. Is there a program

nearby?"

"There is a vocational vet-tech program at a community college. Maybe I should check it out."

She smiles. "Let's go see Goose."

When I get to the back where the kennels are located, I call softly, "Goose, are you back here?"

I hear his tail thumping against the kennel floor and a slight whining.

"Oh, Goose, how are you man?" Judith opens the kennel door and helps me get the dog out and on the floor. He curls around my feet. I notice his IV line is out. "Is he eating?"

"He is. I'm giving him just a little soft, canned food about every other hour, and he is drinking. He is still getting some pain meds in the form of drops. Tomorrow we can give him a bath."

I'm so pleased. His brown eyes are beginning to sparkle again. After we pet him, Judith helps me get him back in the kennel.

Back in the reception area, I ask what I owe them on his bill.

"Doc hasn't given me the charges yet. I'll let you know when you pick him up. Hey Lora, could you go to lunch one day? It gets kind of isolated out here."

"Oh, sure. I'm doing a little work for the Sheriff's

Department right now. I don't think I'm going in on Monday. Do you want to meet me somewhere?"

We agreed on a little café not far from her office. Since I genuinely like Judith, I feel a little guilty about listening for new information. But if this case works out like I think it will, it might be a blessing for her and maybe a new friend for me.

CHAPTER 29
Sam

Now that I know Goose has a good chance of recovery, I can get my head straightened out. There is so much going through my brain, sometimes it's hard to sleep. I want these first few months of married life to be full of sweet memories.

We both loved our monster hunt. I've got to get back to my seventh-graders with the proposed monster project. They seemed interested in something for the first time this school year.

I'm also admitting to myself that we are cramped for space. Two people and a big dog make my two-room cabin seem pretty tight. Maybe I should swallow my pride and reconsider Helen's offer of letting us stay in her big cabin on the water.

Maybe this Friday night would be a good time to go to Mrs. Josie's store and listen to some good mountain music.

It would be great if Goose feels good enough to go. Even though he is still sore, he will want to run around and visit. We will see how he feels when we get him home.

That first time that I took Lora there and we sat in the bed of the truck, wrapped in a blanket, looking at the stars, was the night I thought she might be the one.

Yep. That's what we need—music, friends, food cooked in cast iron vessels in the night air, and each other.

CHAPTER 30
Lora

When I get to the vet's office, Judith is smiling like she can't wait for me to see Goose. She goes to the back and brings him out on a leash. He is all wiggles and wags.

"Looks like you and Doc have worked a miracle."

"Oh, no. Just a little fluids, meds and yummy canned food. You'll need to keep him on this another day or two while his stitches dissolve." She hands me a sack with three cans of dog food and his medication.

"Hey, man, how are you?" I pat his head and look with amazement at how good his coat looks. His mouth is still a little swollen, making him look like he is pouting.

"I'm afraid to ask about the bill, Judith. Tell me what I owe you."

She flips through his chart and finds the statement. Looks like $300. We didn't charge you board last night. We were just feeding him and babysitting."

"Oh, thanks. Can you hold him while I get my checkbook?"

I hand her the leash and go back to the car to get my purse. As I write the check I wonder where this money is going to come from. Maybe my Sheriff's Department check will come in soon.

"Hey Lora," says Judith. "Do you still want to meet for lunch Monday?"

"Sure. I need to make sure I'm not working that day. I'll call you back when I know for sure."

Goose is feeling so good that he is a little hard for me to handle as I get him out the door and into the back seat of Sam's truck.

"Okay, boy. I'm taking you home. You have disrupted our lives for too long." When I look at him in the rear-view mirror, he is smiling a lopsided dog grin thanks to the stitches pulling on one side of his mouth.

After I get him settled, I make a trip to town to talk to Will Jackson.

Claudia ushers me into his office and closes the door.

"Thanks for seeing me Will. I have something I wanted to tell you about. I may be making too many assumptions. From what I can tell, your search in the past for Marian was more of a recovery mission for a body. Would you say that's true?"

"At first, they approached it as a rescue, according to what I was told. When she had been gone two weeks, I think the they took the recovery route—but got no results. Why do you ask?"

"I'm searching for a person instead. And I might have found her, right here under our noses."

Will sat there for a while just looking at me like I had two heads. He finally responded. "What has made you come to that conclusion, Lora?'

"At this point, it is just a theory." I told him about Judith and the background similarities.

"There will still be so many questions…..who took her, where is that family now, where is her real family. I'm having lunch with her next Monday. I really like her. To be safe, I wanted to ask her a few questions."

"If you are discreet. If there is enough evidence, I'll have to question her—at her home or here in the office. Remember, she is not suspected of any wrong doing."

"Oh, absolutely not. Should I bring Claudia?"

"Not yet. Check in with me after your lunch."

By the way, where did you find her?"

"She works for the local veterinarian Dr. Mitchell Granger. Her name is Judith Cole."

The sheriff pauses for a minute. "I think I know who you are talking about. We had to take our dog out there to get her spayed. You never know, right?"

"That's true. Thanks, Sheriff." Claudia eyes me suspiciously when I emerge from the office. "Hey, Claudia. Want to go organize more of our paperwork at the church? Maybe Friday?"

"Sure. Meet you at the church?"

"Sounds good."

"Claudia," says Will. "Can you get me any information on a Judith Cole? She works at the vet office. She's not a person of interest but see if you can find a birth certificate or any other public records."

I hurry home to see Sam and see how his class

reacted to the monster tales and local lore being introduced into their boring history class.

CHAPTER 31
Sam

"Okay, guys. I asked you to write on a note card some of your experiences with the legends of monsters and ghosts in West Virginia. You may not have any. You may not believe in any of this. That's okay too. So, if you have those please pass them to the front. I'm not going to read them out loud. This just gives me an idea of what you think."

Students passed their cards to the person on the front row and I picked them up and casually dropped them in my satchel. We continued with our usual lesson plan.

Before being dismissed, I told them that we would start talking about the legends and lore at the next class. It was hard to read their expressions.

When I got home, I spent some time looking

through the notecards. Some were signed and some not. I promised not to reveal who wrote the card, but I would read them out loud and then we would discuss them.

J.W. My granddaddy used to tell us that Chief Cornstalk had cursed the area of Point Pleasant.

My response: *What do you think about this? Tell us next time more about Chief Cornstalk. Was this before or after the sightings of the Mothman were reported?*

M.S. My parents and grandparents never talked about this stuff. I don't like it. It scares me.

My response: *What scares you about it? Are you interested in learning more about the first settlers coming to these mountains and how many of these legends got started?*

N.H. I asked my great-uncle, who is in his 80s, and he told me about the ghosts of the peddlers. But he didn't know much about it.

My response: *According to my resource in Morgantown, Dr. Cutland, peddlers' ghosts were popular in West Virginia. These were murdered peddlers who came back for revenge. These stories served as warnings against killing peddlers. Peddlers were popular victims because they carried cash and were strangers. They were good for the local economies and* *residents as potentially the sole source for manufactured goods.*

Wow. That's only three cards and 15 to go. My responses here are just ideas. I hope it will spur some discussion and discourage any fear on the subject.

Goose is here at my feet. Surely feels good to have him home. I think I hear Lora driving up. That will make things even better.

She walks in, tired but smiling. Seeing her still makes my heart flutter a little. Dropping her satchel, she plops down on the couch beside me and leans in for a kiss.

"You smell like school," she says.

"Is that bad?" I ask, sniffing the sleeve of my shirt.

"Nope. Just school smell. You know that pencil, cafeteria, disinfectant school smell? I love it, cause it tells me you are here."

Another kiss.

"Hey, don't get carried away. Guess what today is."

"Friday," she says.

"Yep. And if it's Friday, that means Friday night at the store. Can I have a date?"

"You bet." She rests her head on my shoulder.

CHAPTER 32
Lora

I call Judith and we agree to meet as planned at the little café, known for its homemade pies with mile-high meringue.

We arrive about the same time in front of what was once an old country store, much like Mrs. Josie's. The worn, wooden planks of the front porch creak and groan as we step on them. Inside are antique glass-front display cases, full of pies, cakes and other pastries.

Sodas are iced down in old RC Cola open coolers, right by the cash register. It would be hard to check out without letting your hand dive down deep in the vat of ice and water and see what kind of bottled soda you come up with.

It's 11:30, so maybe we are ahead of the regular

lunch crowd. The simple menu is written on a chalk board behind the counter. So we order—a pimiento cheese sandwich for me, with a side of homemade potato salad. Instead of taking the icy drink dive, I order a sweet tea with lemon. They actually have it.

Judith has a sandwich piled high with thin sliced roasted chicken, cheese, and a homemade sauce. It's a specialty of the restaurant. She dives for a bottled 7-Up.

We take our seats at a small picnic table covered with a red and white tablecloth. I'm glad we are near the back of the place so we can talk.

"This all looks so good," I say adding a dash of black pepper to my sandwich. "It reminds me of another country store that I'm pretty fond of. By the way, they have music at Mrs. Josie's store every Friday night. People sit on blankets or the beds of their trucks, eat great food, and listen to music. You can bring something or purchase something that's cooked over the fire. It's great. You should come."

"Maybe," says Judith. "So, what are you doing for the Sheriff's Department—if you can talk about it?" she asks.

That question right off the bat catches me a little off guard. "It's a cold case involving a missing girl. That's about all I can talk about right now."

"Oh, I understand," she says as she straightens her silverware. It's always a little awkward when you begin a friendship. I tell her about our farm in Mississippi, and how I met Sam the first day I was here.

She is interested in the grant work I did when I first arrived in West Virginia. I compared cultural similarities between the Appalachians and the rural South.

"Funding ran out, and I had to decide whether to stay here or go home. But there was Sam. My daddy died suddenly, and when I went home for the funeral, I took Sam to see how he would like Mississippi."

"How did that go?" said Judith as she carefully cut her sandwich into triangles.

"It was good. He seemed to fit in, and liked my family, and my old family farm house, and the dogs and horses. When he willingly added our names to our carving tree, I knew we were on track."

"What's a carving tree?" she asked pausing with her knife in mid-air.

"We have an American Beech tree on our land. Our ancestors have carved on it for 100 years. You can barely make out some of the signatures. Since Sam is a carver, our names were the most beautifully-carved on the tree. Then I knew."

"So, what about you? Have you always lived in West Virginia?"

"I have. My real parents died when I was really young, and I went to live with my mother's cousin in a small town not far from here. She and her husband adopted me. I don't remember much about my first parents or my home with them."

"You've had a good life with your cousin, I hope?" I ask, trying not to pry too much.

"Oh yes, the best. I was happy with them. I brought Shep with me, and he lived to be about 12, which is a long time for a big dog. I finished high school and started college. There I met this guy I thought I couldn't live without. Turned out that he could live without me. I haven't remarried, and we didn't have children."

Maybe I had asked too many nosey questions for the first time spending some time with her. I'll have to drop back and make some more ordinary conversation.

"Tell me about Mississippi," Judith says, pinching off small pieces of her chicken sandwich. I get the idea she is not very hungry.

Well, if you ask me that question, you just have to wind me up and sit back and listen. When I looked at my watch, I realized I had rambled on for 30 minutes.

"Oh, dear. I've almost talked through the whole lunch hour. Did we want to try the pie?"

"I would love some, but we might have to get it to go. I need to get back to the clinic."

"Pie is my treat," I offer. She chooses coconut cream, and I get chocolate fudge to take to Sam, and old-fashioned chess pie for me.

We said our goodbyes, and I got the feeling she might enjoy another visit. I wonder how long before I should tell her about my side job and what I'm really looking for.

CHAPTER 33
Will

It's hard to believe that Lora might have a lead on this case so soon. I've had Claudia doing research at the courthouse and at the Department of Records at the State for a few days.

She was able to find a birth certificate for a Judith Redding. No Judith Cole. This child would be the same age as Marian and was born here in the county to Wilson and Sharon Redding.

There was also a birth certificate for Marian Atchley, born to John and Mira Atchley. There was also a death certificate that had been issued for Marian Atchley.

According to West Virginia law, when death is presumed to have occurred within the state, but the body cannot be located, a certificate of death may be prepared by the state. The registrar must receive an order of a court of competent jurisdiction which shall include the finding of facts required to complete the certificate of death.

Claudia found court records showing the evidence of death to be the sudden disappearance of the child and the finding of a tattered dress material with blood stains found near the Atchley cabin. After a more than reasonable search and a period of 5 years had passed, the certificate was issued bringing closure to the family.

All we have been able to find out about the Atchleys is that they were shown in the 1970 census in nearby Ripley.

The Reddings were shown on the same census in 1970, living out in the county from Elizabeth. Wilson Redding was listed as a part-time miner and self-employed craftsman. Sharon Redding showed her occupation as a clerk in a local department store. Their daughter Judith Redding was listed as a student, aged 16.

So what theories can we derive from this information. I think it's time for Lora and me to talk to Judith. It will be hard.

CHAPTER 34
Lora

I get a call from Will telling me it's time to talk to Judith. I try to get mentally prepared to make this call, but I haven't had the nerve yet. Later today, I tell myself.

After lunch at our cabin, I call Judith.

"Vet Clinic," she says when she answers the phone.

"Hey, Judith. It's Lora. Are you busy?"

"Not right now. What's up?"

"You remember my telling you I was doing a little research for the Sheriff's Department?"

"Sure."

"Sheriff Jackson and I think that you might shed some light on this case we are investigating. Would you be able to come talk to us one afternoon this week?"

"Me?" she asked with surprise in her voice. "What is the case about? How could I help?"

"We have some documents we want you to look at and help us identify some of the people in them."

"Well, okay." She is hesitant. I knew she would be. "I think Doc is closing early tomorrow. I could come about 2:30. Would that work?"

"That's great. See you at the Sheriff's office. Thank for helping us out on this."

"I hope I can help. I can't imagine what I might know about this case."

"We'll see you tomorrow."

When I hang up, my heart is racing. I hope we don't offend her. I also hope I don't lose a friend in the process.

CHAPTER 35
Will

It's almost time for our meeting with Judith Cole. I have a list of questions, and I'm sure Lora does too. I don't want to intimidate Judith or make her feel like she has done something wrong. We just need to know if she is, in fact, Marian Atchley.

Lora comes in the door with Judith behind her. They must have met in the parking area. I know Claudia wants to be involved, too. Maybe not today, but definitely in the future.

"Hi, Judith. I'm Will Jackson. Thanks for coming to meet with us. Let's go in here in the records room. I cleared the table so we would have some room to look at a few things."

I can tell that Judith is nervous. Her hands shake as she puts down a legal pad to take notes.

"Judith don't be nervous about this little meeting. We just need to clear up an old case, and Lora thinks you might be able to help us."

"I can't imagine……" she says, shaking her head. Clearly, my words did nothing to calm her nerves.

Lora started the explanation of the meeting. "Judith, let me tell you about the case I've been working on. It involves the case of a missing little girl. She lived with her family up around Curly Willow Creek. Are you familiar with that area?"

"I know where it is," says Judith.

Lora continues. "This little girl was outside her parent's cabin, playing with her new puppy—a shepherd mix. When the mother looked out to check on her just 10 minutes later, she was gone. But the puppy was still there."

I searched Judith's face to see if I saw any reaction. There was none.

"Marian's parents were John and Mira Atchley," I tell her. "We think they left this area around 1964. Through national databases, we found a death certificate for John, but not Mira. After five years Marian was declared dead, and a death certificate was issued."

Lora patted Judith's hand for reassurance. "Are you still wondering what all this has to do with you?" Judith nodded.

"I want to show you something before we go any further." I reach in the file cabinet behind me and pull out the old clipping file. I thumb through the clippings until I see the paper with the front-page story on the missing girl along with a photo.

I slide it across the table to Judith. "Anything about that look familiar?"

Judith puts her hand to her mouth and tears spring to her eyes. She looks up at me in disbelief. "That's me! Am I Marian Atchley?"

"We believe you might be," says Lora.

We take a break and allow Judith time to go through the clippings. She has an intensely-disturbed look on her face as she reads each one. Lora and I have left her alone to go through these documents that could change who she is and open a new perspective on her past.

An hour later, she emerges from the room. "Sheriff Jackson, Lora, I don't know what to say. Is there more information you haven't told me?"

"There are more questions, Judith," I tell her.

She looks miserable. "I need to go get some air—

maybe go get something to drink. I feel like my heart is coming out of my chest."

"Sure," says Lora. "Why don't you go down to the coffee shop a few doors down and take a break. I can come with you or you can go alone."

"Why don't you come with me Lora, unless we are not supposed to discuss the case without the Sheriff being present."

"It's okay if you two go alone," I tell her. "However, if you discuss anything that would add to the findings of this case, Lora is to report that to me. Understand?"

"Of course."

When Lora and Judith go out the door, Claudia motions me over to her desk.

"Look what I found." She shows me her computer screen. "You might want to sit down."

I pull up one of the old wooden office chairs and read over her shoulder.

"I looked at records in the county where John Atchley's death was reported. I found a phone number for a M. Stanfield-Atchley. She was in the 1990 census.

Guess I didn't pick it up on the first search because the name was hyphenated and filed under S. Her address in the most recent phone book corresponds with a retirement community. According to the 1990 census she would now be a 72-years-old.

"I searched for a birth certificate for Mira Stanfield and there she is again. Age and race are a match. We may have found Marian-Judith's birth mother."

"Good work, Claudia. You're my hero. Let's not mention this to Judith until we get more verification. Is this an assisted living facility?"

"No, more of a subdivision of small homes from what I can tell. They do have an office and a manager. Some qualify for home health checks."

"Claudia, can you call that office and see if Mira still lives there and get some idea of her condition, mental and physical. I may have to ride over there and pay her a visit."

CHAPTER 36
Will

I get a call from Claudia telling me that she
talked to the manager of the retirement community
where Mira lives. She has been a resident there
for about three years. According to the manager,
Mira is in relatively good health and considerably
younger than most of the others in the community.
She moved there after living alone following her
husband's death.

She still drives, volunteers at the library and is
in good health except for aches and pains that come
with age. She told the manager, she just wanted a
new start after her husband died. Here, she wouldn't
have a yard to worry about mowing.

Claudia asked the manager if she thought Mira
would be up to answering questions about her

daughter who disappeared in 1959. She thought it would be okay. So, she made me an appointment, and I'm on my way there now.

So many questions are running around in my head. I don't want to scare her. We need to be sure that Judith is Marian, so I don't get her hopes up for nothing.

I pull up in front of her little apartment, surrounded by dozens of others just like it. It's a nice little community with a walking track at the center of the apartments. Landscapers keep the border neatly-planted with seasonal flowers and perennial ground cover.

I knock on the door. It is opened by an attractive woman who wears her silver hair in a pony tail, high on her head. She doesn't look like I might have expected her to. Her casual jeans and dangling silver earrings make her look younger than she is.

"Mrs. Atchley? I'm Sheriff Will Jackson. I think we have an appointment."

"Yes, Sheriff. Please, come in. I am extremely curious about why you are here. Please come sit down."

"I understand that your daughter, Marian, disappeared in 1959, correct?"

"Yes. I never gave up hope of finding her. After

she was legally declared dead, I had to get out of our house in your county. There were too many reminders. My husband never got over it, and we never had other children."

"I am particularly interested in this case because my dad, Frank Jackson, was sheriff during that time. He never got over it either. He never could understand how she could disappear in the blink of an eye, with no clues, no evidence, no witnesses."

"Could it be that you have now found something," she asks, her hands beginning to shake.

"Maybe. I need to ask you some questions first, if you don't mind." She nods, so I continue. "Take me back to the morning she disappeared. Tell me step-by-step what you remember."

Mira Atchley tells me the same story that I've read in police reports, in newspapers—the same story she told my dad in 1959. She never wavers.

"Do you have any early photographs of Marian that you could show me?"

"Yes, I do. Let me get them," she says.

Mira goes to one of the rooms in the back of the apartment and returns with a tattered, but beautiful keepsake box.

"I have a few photographs. We were so poor back then; we didn't have much of anything."

I go through the pictures, some familiar, that I'd seen in the paper. And one of Marian and her dog. I pay close attention to the collar. It's just a plain brown collar.

"Was Marian a shy girl? Would she have been terrified at going with someone she knew?"

"No, probably not. She was friendly—never met a stranger. Maybe I should have cautioned her more."

"Did you ever think she might have known the person who took her, if that is what happened? Neither my dad, other officers, nor I saw any evidence that she had suffered an accident. We would have eventually found her."

Mira looks down and touches the things in her box. "This is hard for me, Sheriff. Any more questions?"

"Well, here is what we have found." I tell her about the scrap of dress material with the blood on it, and about hiring Lora Wood to go back through old documents and compare them with the documents recently found in the church. Then I relate how Lora met Judith Redding Cole at the local vet office.

"She told Lora she was adopted and lived with her mother's cousin and her husband (Jeff and

Sharon Redding), and had a shepherd-mix dog as a child."

I told her that we had interviewed Judith and showed her the old newspaper clipping.

"When I showed her the photo in the paper," I said, reaching for one of the photos in the box and holding it up, "she positively identified the girl as herself."

Mira did not move, but tears began to stream down her face.

"I'll give you a moment and then I need to ask a few more questions."

She sits back down.

"Do you know Wilson and Sharon Redding?"

"They went to the Curly Willow Church, but I didn't really know them."

"Did they have a child?"

"Yes, a little girl about Marian's age."

"Did Marian ever play with their daughter?"

"Only at church. Sharon helped with Sunday School for about a month. Then they quit coming to church, as I remember. But that was about the time we lost Marian, so some things are just a blur."

"Do you or your husband know how to braid or plait leather or string?"

"No. What an unusual question."

"It has bearing on this case. Did Marian practice braiding?"

"Yes, she did. In fact, as I recall, she said Mrs. Redding let them practice braiding during craft time at Sunday School. They made a Bible bookmark. I think Mr. Redding was a leather craftsman."

"Did you ever see the dog after Marian disappeared?"

"No."

"Where did she get the puppy?"

"He just showed up at the house one day."

"Why did you go through the process of having her declared dead?"

"That was my husband's idea. We had lost a child but had no funeral. No friends coming by to say how sorry they were, no grave. It just gave him some closure. There was no legal reason why."

I'm not sure she is ready for my theory, but I have strong enough evidence that I feel safe sharing it with her. The last thing I want to do is get her hopes up only to crush her again.

"I believe that somehow Sharon formed a bond with your daughter. We talked to their neighbor and he told us that their daughter died, but there is no death certificate. No record of their living here in this county can be found after 1959. But there are records of Judith Redding on the 1960 census, and she shows up in school records.

"Mira, we think that when their daughter Judith died, they took Marian and changed her identity. You could do things like that during that time period that would be harder to do today.

"Both Sharon and Wilson Redding are listed as deceased, and Judith verifies that. Since you tell me that they had a connection to the church, that tells me two things: that she knew Marian, and that she could have access to store the information she had in the church tower. She may have felt like it shouldn't be in her possession in case anyone tied her to the kidnapping."

"What happened to their child?"

"We still aren't sure on that one," I say. "She could have died of natural causes and they just buried her. Maybe they knew she was sick and had already started thinking about the substitution. We can't prove foul play without a body or death certificate. I have my staff searching for relatives to question."

"What about the blood on the dress material?"

"We aren't sure. We didn't want to ask Judith about it until we talked to you, but I don't think she came to any harm, if that is any comfort. She told us that she vaguely remembers going to live with Reddings, who she considered to be your cousins. She may remember more than she realizes. We can find that out through counseling.

"Where is she now?"

"She works in a veterinarian's office in Elizabeth, about an hour from here. She told Lora that she was married, hence the last name Cole, but the marriage didn't last but about five years."

"Is it time for me to meet her?"

"Not quite." Her excitement fades away.

Mira gets up and moved around the kitchen and then disappeared to the bedroom of the apartment.

"Prove this to me," she said, handing me a small lock of hair tied with a blue ribbon and pressed together between sheets of wax paper. "This is all of her I have."

CHAPTER 37
Lora

After meeting with Mira, Will calls a meeting with Claudia and me.

"I think we are getting very close to closing the file on this case," says Will, taking a sip of coffee from his favorite coffee-stained mug.

"We need to wait until the DNA testing comes back from the state. At that point, if we have a positive match, we need to get Mira and Judith together. Maybe they can fill in some holes."

"Like what caused the blood on the dress," added Claudia. "Those are things that only Judith can tell us. She may have blocked all that out."

"She may have just fallen down, running in the woods with the dog and tore her dress," I suggest.

"There is no evidence that she was purposely harmed."

"I also feel like maybe after Marian/Judith and Sharon Redding had bonded, that Redding was sneaking over there to see her and they practiced braiding—first a three plait, then a four, and finally the five plait like the collar on the dog," says Will. "She probably gave her the puppy as a lure."

"How long before the test comes back?" I asked.

"Maybe by the end of the week, maybe next week," says Claudia. "Several days at least."

"I say that we let this settle in with the two women. After the test comes back, we can arrange a meeting. Both of you did outstanding work on this case," says Will.

Meeting adjourned.

I go home. I'm looking forward to getting this off my mind and giving Sam the attention he deserves. After all, we have only been married a month.

CHAPTER 38
Sam

Goose and I are sitting on my little front porch. He knows it's about time for Lora to come home. He looks at the road and then back at me, thumping his tail.

The woods around the cabin are coming alive. The trees are budding out with those fresh green leaves. Birds are singing. I have a pretty good feeling inside.

I'm glad Lora took on this side job of searching for Marian Atchley. It gave her something to do and a little income. Seems we have been searching ever since we got married in early March. First, we searched for monsters. I'm so glad we did this. It was fun and a little creepy too.

I captured the attention of my hard-to-reach

seventh graders. That's a hard group to reach. By telling them about the ghosts and monsters, they accidentally learned something about our state—the immigrants who settled here and the myths and legends they brought with them.

It also gave the kids a chance to open up and tell me about their own monsters. More of the students than I realized lived in bad home situations. Some of them told me about that. They know that I'm somebody they can come talk to. Their situations gave me insight as to why they didn't do their homework, why they acted out in class, and why many had that dead look in their eyes like they had no hope. It was worth the trip.

And then there was the hunt for Goose. I still don't know exactly how he got trapped in that old cabin. It was obvious that he was hurt with his whole mouth full of porcupine quills.

Then Lora started her search for Marian. Looks like they are near the end of that mystery.

It's April now, school will be out in about six weeks. I feel a trip to Mississippi is in our future. Lora has been gone long enough now. Goose perks up. She must be turning onto our road.

CHAPTER 39
Lora

I have just crawled out of bed and shuffled to the kitchen to let Goose out. Before I even have time to start the coffee pot, my phone rings.

"Lora? Will Jackson here. Sorry to call so early, but I wanted to give you some news. The state has certified that the DNA on the dress and the hair sample that Mira Atchley gave me are a match. Judith is Marian."

My throat closes and it's hard to get a word out.

"I want to set up a meeting with Judith and Mira. Do you think you can get Judith to come down to the office about 11 this morning?"

"I'll try. Do you want me to tell her or wait until we get together at the office?"

"Let's wait. We don't know how she will react, or Mira, for that matter. If Mira can come, I'll go get her and bring her to the office. Make the phone call, please and let me know ASAP so I know how to proceed."

I call Judith and ask her to meet me at the office at 11. I can't get a good read on whether she will consider this good news or bad. She agrees to the meeting.

When Judith arrives at the office, she is visibly nervous. I give her a hug, and we go to the little records room where we met before.

"Can you tell me what this is about?"

"Not yet. When Sheriff Jackson gets here we can brief you on what's going on."

We make small talk. She asks about Goose and how he is doing.

Claudia comes in and joins us.

"Judith, this is Officer Watson. She has been working on this case for some time. In fact, she had just joined the staff here when Marian disappeared. She worked for Will's father, Sheriff Frank Jackson."

We hear the door open. Will flips the closed sign, locks the door, and enters the room with Mira Atchley. The two women look at each other intensely, then look away.

Will starts the conversation. "Judith, Mira, I want to tell you in person that the state has given us the results of the DNA test. There is a 98 percent probability that you, Judith, are Marian Atchley, Mira's daughter."

Both women glance at each other, and tears began to stream silently down their faces. Will goes over the whole progression of the investigation that led to our solving this cold case.

"Why don't we give you some time to process this," he says. "We do have a few questions, which can be answered whenever you are ready."

I give them a smile, Claudia pats them both on the shoulders, and we all leave the room. When I look back, Mira and her daughter have reached across the table and are holding hands in silence.

EPILOGUE

It took some time, but Mira and Judith (Marian) finally opened up to each other. Together they found missing pieces of the puzzle. After some counseling for Judith, she realized that she did have some memories of her early childhood, and they were good ones.

Mira showed her old family photographs. "You have my mother's eyes. Don't you think?" Judith had noticed that before Mira pointed it out.

When Judith crossed her legs, Mira noticed a deep scar on her right knee.

"What caused the scar," she asked, afrait she was prying.

"I was running with Shep and fell on a sharp rock. I just remember how bad it hurt. That's really all I remember."

Judith bore no real hatred for the Reddings. They had been good to her, but she had a hard time processing what they had done to her real parents.

Weeks after the investigation closed, Sheriff Jackson and his deputies found a small grave near the property the Reddings had owned. After all these years, it was impossible to determine the cause of death. It didn't appear to show any evidence of a homicide. The grave was marked only by a small stone. Their property was secluded, and the little grave had gone undisturbed all these years. The real Judith Redding's remains were moved to the town cemetery.

Judith had her name legally changed to Marian Judith Atchley. She dropped the last name of Cole since it belonged to her ex-husband and brought only memories of a union of two kids who married too young. Judith and Mira Atchley worked at mending a relationship torn apart. She and Lora remained friends.

Will Jackson decided to throw his hat back in the ring when the time came for county elections. Officer Claudia Watson was named investigator and given a big raise just a year before her retirement.

Lora and Sam started all over with their marriage which had been interrupted from the beginning.

They continued to live in Sam's cabin, but were considering adding to their family. When that happened, Sam finally agreed to take Helen up on her offer for them to live in her beautiful and bigger mountain retreat.

Al and Tony finished the heating and air job at the Curly Willow Church. Services there began again, and all documents were moved to the Sheriff's Office.

Rex continued to win his battle with drug addiction, though it was always in the back of his mind. The Friday night muic at the store became a popular destination for folks in the region. Rex and his mother developed a menu as well as a seating area for diners. The store was doing business like it never had before.

Back in Mississippi, Buck and Simsie had a baby girl in the fall. They named her Madison, which is Lora's middle name. Simsie continued her nursing career, Buck kept Sinclair farm up and running, and they worked at renovating the 150-year old farm house.

"Hey Sam, are you glad we did the monster search?" Lora asks as she sits on the deck looking out over the lake.

"Absolutely. In searching for those ghosts and monsters, I may have found a few seventh-graders who needed someone to talk to. That was what I wanted all along."

"Hey Sam," she says, squinting at me with one eye shut. "I need to go home for a while when school is out."

"Well baby, that's only two weeks away. Start packing."

"Are we going to fly?"

"I think so."

"What about Goose?"

"He can stay with Rex."

I sit by her on the deck and brush a loose strand of hair away from her face and kiss her deeply.

"Know what?" I ask.

"No, what."

"Tonight is Friday. Want to go to the store, listen to some music, sit in the back of my truck, and eat West Virginia food cooked outside, just like we did that first date?'

"You bet," she says.

ACKNOWLEDGEMENTS

Sam, Lora, Buck, Simsie, Paulette, Asa, Merry Bell, and the whole cast of characters of these three books: *The Carving Place, The Bargain—Paulette's Story,* and *Finding Marian,* have been running around in my head for three years. They have been my constant companions.

I feel like I should get in an old pickup truck and go to the Sinclair Farm, to the Crossroads Market, to Mrs. Josie's store in West Virginia, to Will Jackson's Sheriff's Office, and to Sam's cabin in the Appalachians.

Though I haven't set foot in West Virginia, I had some great experts to help me with the mountain lore and myths, and the dialect of their state. The character of Dr. Aleida Cutland is based on the real Beth Toren. Read more about her and the other real stars on the next pages.

Thanks to Chad Martin for helping me through the publishing process once again.

BETH TOREN

Beth Toren is an interdisciplinary, cultural and film studies librarian at West Virginia University. When I asked Beth to tell me exactly what she does, this was her response:

"I have wide and eclectic interests. I call myself a Paraphysicist to indicate that I am interested in things that are irreverent to academia, that I don't take myself seriously, and I like the creative, playful, surrealistic approach to science. I earned a master's in Library Science from the University of Kentucky

in Lexington.

"In a previous job title, Media and Research Services Librarian at the WVU Downtown Campus Library, I developed and taught a film and media literacy course covering the subject of rumors, hoaxes and urban legends.

One way I became knowledgeable about West Virginia folklore began with using my art and theater skills to do lots of library displays. There was a new *Men in Black* film and it was very popular. The Men in Black originated in the next town south of Morgantown, Fairmont WV. I did a display case about the Men in Black and "Paranormal West Virginia." *Photo by Brian Persinger*

PATTY WOLFORD

Native West Virginia artist Patty Hendricks Wolford generously gave me permission to use her abstract Mothman drawing on the cover of the book. She grew up along Coal River in Boone County. From early childhood, she longed to create art. She received a degree in Fine Art from Berea College in Kentucky.

Since that time, she has worked in a variety of

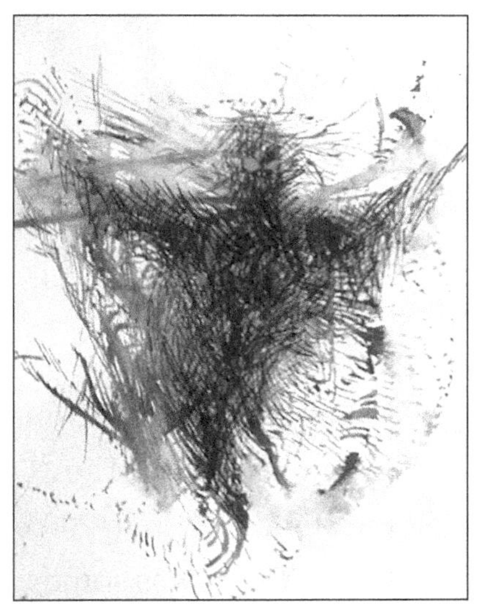

art-related vocations, including cartoonist/illustrator for the State of West Virginia, studio artist at the William King Arts Center in Abington, Va., and public school art teacher in Putnam County, WV.

During her time in Virginia, she was a recipient of the Virginia Governor's Award for the Arts. She completed her M.A. in Art at Marshall University with an emphasis in fiber arts.

"I live in Putnam County, not far from Point Pleasant ," says Wolford. "I like it (the Mothman legend) as a very interesting myth. I also like the history of native Americans as they encountered the early pioneers moving into their territory, where a fort was constructed at Point Pleasant. The killing of Chief Cornstalk at the fort was said to place a curse on the region, perhaps connected to the mothman myth. Also the curse perhaps is the reason Point has never thrived or grown despite being located at the confluence of two major rivers.

JEFF WAMSLEY

Since my story took place in 1998, there is now a Mothman Festival. Jeff Wamsley is the owner of the Mothman Museum which attracts hundreds during the festival and many regular visitors during

the year. The museum started in 2006. The festival began in 2003.

"There was some tourist activity before then (2003) especially with the movie release (*The Mothman Prophecies,* starring Richard Gere and Laura Linney) in 2002," says Wamsley. There are a few living witnesses. Some will talk about their sightings, and some have never spoken about that they saw.

"Most have described what they saw as being seven feet tall, grayish in color, with two distinct red eyes about the size of baseballs. Some saw it at night, while others in the daytime.

"Many take the Mothman as a serious entity and have researched the legend since the '60s.. Some view it as a part of pop culture and almost like Batman or some super hero. Kids seem to love the Mothman just as I did Batman when I was a kid."

Visit the museum at www.mothmanmuseum. com

Wansley poses with the Mothman statue that is near his museum in downtown Point Pleasant. (photo by cryptomundo.com)

NOLAN HARRIS

Cowboy and leather craftsman Nolan Harris of Coldwater, Miss., gave me advice about the specifics of the collar that Shep would have worn. When I asked him what he would use he said, "Let me try it and see how it works."

He didn't get to do that since he was in the hospital at the time, fighting pancreatic cancer and other conditions. My idea of a six-strand, he said, wouldn't work.

"Slip stitch, flat, five strand is what I'd use." Thanks for the help Nolan. There aren't many true leather craftsmen left. Nolan Harris lost his battle with cancer on Easter, April 12, 2020.

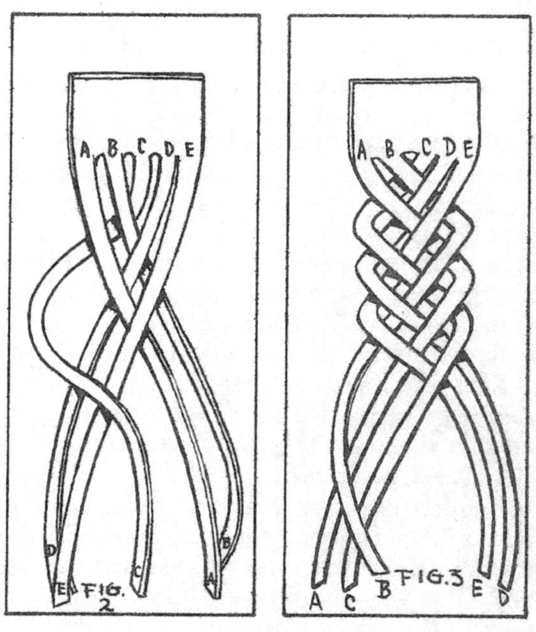

This is one version of a flat five-strand plait as described in Leather Braiding by Bruce Grant, published by Cornell Maritime Press in Centerville, MD, 1950. Illustration is by Larry Spinell. My dad, Hayley Dandridge, was also a leather craftsman. I have seen him consult this book many times.

OTHER SOURCES:

https://en.wikipedia.org/wiki/Mothman

https://en.wikipedia.org/wiki/Flatwoods_
monster

https://wvtourism.com/5-of-the-most-haunted-
locations-in-west-virginia/

https://magazine.wvu.edu/
stories/2016/10/28/flashback-haunted-halls

https://www.thelowehotel.com

https://www.hillspet.com/dog-care/
healthcare/dogs-and-porcupine-quills

https://www.history.com/news/men-in-black-
real-origins

Journal Entry
A season to remember, Spring 2020

On the heels of one of the grayest and wettest winters that I remember, came a force that had global impact. The Novel Coronavirus was first reported in China in December 2019.

In February, a man in the Philippines died—the first death reported outside the mainland of China. The virus began to spread.

Also in February a Royal Caribbean Cruise ship set said from Bayonne, New Jersey, after a coronavirus scare had kept it docked for days. It began to travel, and we watched on television and on computers the reports of the virus spreading throughout Europe.

President Donald Trump appointed Vice President Mike Pence to head the task force response team to deal with the coronavirus. Finally cases were reported in the United States.

One by one, states declared a state of emergency. The stock market plunged.

And finally in March, in Senatobia, Mississippi, I felt the virus changing the way of life in this small

Southern town. One day it was announced there was a case in Mississippi, three days later there were 50. It was mutating and spreading faster than anything we had seen before.

Shoppers here followed a national trend to head to local grocery and dollar stores for toilet paper, cleaning supplies, and sanitizer of any kind. Shelves were empty. Then the run was on for meat. Shoppers hoarded package after package of fresh meat into their carts.

Miss. Gov. Tate Reeves announced the closing of all public school through April 17, possibly for the end of the semester.

Private schools, colleges, and universities followed suit. Educations were forced to come up with distance learning options to keep students from falling behind.

Churches cancelled corporate worship services and delivered their messages online. Doctors' offices screened patients at their front doors and sent them back to their cars to wait until they were ready to be seen by a practitioner.

Hospitals no longer allowed family members to stay with their loved one in the hospital. Waiting rooms for ER and ICU were empty.

The procedures changed daily. Nearby Oxford,

reported that the famous square filled with restaurants and bars, was dark. Square Books closed its doors to walk-in customers but continued to fill mail orders. Senatobia fast-food restaurants filled drive-thru orders only.

President Trump finally asked that no gatherings of 10 or more people meet.

But in all that gloom, families played games, told stories, cooked, read, and actually spent time together. As the rain continued, it was hard for cooped-up children to get rid of cabin fever. When the weather did break, we all rushed outside to escape.

Out of frustration, parents put kids to work making homemade crafts, playing games, working puzzles, and anything else they could think of to keep them busy.

The Teddy bears started popping up around town for the same reason. Parents would ride their children around neighborhoods and look for the Teddy bears in the windows. They played and game to see how many they could spot.

In early April Miss. Gov. Tate Reeves declared a shelter-in-place order. All businesses except those considered essential, such as pharmacies, medical facilities, and grocery stores, were ordered to close. Grocery stores allowed only a few people at a time into their stores. The number allowed in corresponded with square footage of the store.

In a press briefing April 5, President Trump and his advisers said that parts of the country were nearing a peak in cases of coronavirus. U.S. Surgeon General Jerome M. Adams warned that the coming weeks could be a national catastrophe comparable to Pearl Harbor or the Sept. 11, 2001 terrorist attacks.

News anchors reported the daily updates from the safety of their own homes.

The curve has begun to flatten, as of this writing in late April. We are nowhere near our "normal." Economists, social experts, elected officials predict that it will be a long, long time, if ever, that we return to that former state. Small businesses are taking the worst hit.

President Trump has defined steps to gradually open up the country. So far, that has not happened. Here in Mississippi, Gov. Reeves has announced that students will not return to their schools this semester, but that learning will continue through various types of distance learning.

Almost all people you meet who are brave enough to go out shopping for groceries and supplies are wearing masks and gloves.

This week we saw some states start the gradual reopening. Precautions such as wearing masks and practicing social distancing are still in place.

I have to stop with this journal now so that I can send this book to press.

As we wait out this isolated period in our lives, we are reminded of priorities. And we are thankful for the simple things in our lives and for the people we love. God Bless!

—NDP April 2020

https://kvia.com/health/2020/03/19/wuhan-coronavirus-timeline-fast-facts/

ABOUT THE AUTHOR
Nancy Dandridge Patterson

Nancy Dandridge Patterson, a native Tate Countian, retired after a 37-year career in broadcasting and public relations. In 2010 she completed 33 years at Northwest Mississippi Community College where she was serving as director of Public Relations.

Before her PR work, Patterson managed the col-

lege's National Public Radio-affiliated radio station.
She has also worked in small-market radio in Her-
nando, Greenwood, and Holly Springs.

Since retirement, she fulfilled a life-long goal
of learning to quilt. After mastering the basics,
she found her niche in folk-style original-pattern
quilts that tell a story. She has also written for area
newspapers and regional magazines.

A life-long equestrienne, Patterson has enjoyed

showing Appaloosa and Quarter Horses. She took a 13-year break from horseback riding, and in 2015 she began trail riding.

She and her friends and youngest daughter ride at state parks in Mississippi, Tennessee, and in the Arkansas Ozark mountains

Nancy and her husband, Howard, are the parents of three grown children and have four grandchildren. They reside on family farmland in Barr, in Eastern Tate County—where the real carving tree stands tall in their woods.

Finding Marian is the third book in *The Carving Place* series. It is available from local shops in Senatobia and from national booksellers. Books are $12 each or $10 each when you buy two or the entire set.

The author is available for book talks. Send requests or book orders to her at thecarvingplace@gmail.com.